Raven's Dyke

Also in the Series

West Country Tales

   A Rooftop View
   A Marriage of Inconvenience
   Looking for Henry
   Godmother's Footsteps
   Lies and Consequences
   Stormclouds
   Haste to the Wedding
   Things that Go Bump in the Night
   A Different View
   Winds of Change
   Time to Say Goodbye
   Full Circle

   Also by Jane Hatton
   A Dream of Dragons

RAVEN'S DYKE

Jane Hatton

Copyright © Jane Hatton 1978
First published 1978
by William Collins, Sons & Co Ltd under the name Jane Martin
Reprinted by RaJe Publications 2022
Garth Cottage, Little in Sight
Mawnan Smith, Falmouth, TR11 5EY

Distributed by Lightning Source worldwide

The right of Jane Hatton to be identified as the author of the work has been asserted herein in accordance with the Copyright, Designs and Patents Act 1988.

All rights reserved. This book is sold subject to the condition that it shall not, by way of trade or otherwise, be lent, resold, hired out or otherwise circulated without the publisher's prior consent in any form of binding or cover other than that in which it is published and without a similar condition including this condition being imposed on the subsequent purchaser.

All the characters in this book are fictitious and any resemblance to actual people, living or dead, is purely imaginary.

British Library Cataloguing in Publication Data
A catalogue record for this book is available from the British Library

ISBN 978-1-8380372-3-9

Cover design by Amolibros, Milverton, Somerset
www.amolibros.com
This book production has been managed by Amolibros
Printed and bound by Lightning Source worldwide

About the author

Jane Hatton was a child during World War II, and grew up in the unpermissive fifties, when career options for women were largely confined to Secretary, Nurse, Teacher, Physiotherapist. She opted for the first, thinking the skills required would be useful in her preferred career as a writer, but has also worked in hotels, as a sailing instructor, in a craft workshop and as a cookery demonstrator – a remarkably unstructured career – while continuing to write whenever there was a spare moment: sometimes there were not many! She has had two children's books published in the mainstream (a while ago now), followed by three novels in the genre of "literary fiction", plus The One Too Awful to Mention – which we don't mention – and has also independently published a long series about the Nankervis family and their friends and relations, all set in various areas of the West Country. Apart from writing, her interests include sailing, painting – including at one time scenery for the local pantomime – archaeology, photography and cooking. She lives in Cornwall, on her own these days, with a small black cat for company and a background of family and friends.

Author's Note

This book was first published by William Collins & Sons in 1978, written under my then name of Jane Martin, and in the intervening years I had – almost – forgotten about it.

It was always my favourite of my early works, but it was set in yesterday's times, not today's. Then one day, when I was idling about in my study, I took it from the shelf and riffled through it and suddenly realised – hang on, I know these people! And so I did, and so my present readers will too – they appear in several of my later works! After so many years, the original contract with Collins has expired, and on reading it through properly I decided to give it a new look and add it to the present series. It meant revising one or two things – they were still sending telegrams in the original version! – and scattering one or two iPads and computers about the place, but here it is, updated and good to go!

By the time we meet the principal characters again, they have two children of school age, so this one slots in right at the beginning, between *A Rooftop View* and *A Marriage of Inconvenience*.

Enjoy!

I

'Let's choose executors, and talk of wills.'
                                Shakespeare: *Richard II*

The two girls sat side by side on the edge of a handsome swimming pool in the garden of their late father's beautiful Beverley Hills residence. Long, cool drinks stood on a tray between them, and all around them were the trappings of wealth and luxurious living. In spite of these advantages, the younger, Austine, looked as if she had cried for a week, which was very nearly the truth. She was just seventeen, and the bottom had fallen out of her world. The older of the two had not cried more than a very little, but she looked pale and thoughtful and her blue eyes held shadows which had no place there.

They had a problem; however rich and beautiful you may be – and both were rich, and Austine, at least, was beautiful – it is still a tragedy when your life is suddenly cut in two; in the past is family life and love, and the protection of parents – one parent only, in this case, but that one a very special one. Ahead lies…what? A rootless freedom, that from the vantage point of a comfortable and secure home it takes courage to reach out for. Where once there was security, with no need to think about tomorrow, there is now the necessity to grapple with life on your own terms, to look out for yourself and to find your own way. It is something, paradoxically, that is more difficult to do the more fortunate you have been in the past.

When Austin Willerby died, the world of films and theatre mourned for the passing of a very fine actor. His two daughters mourned him on a more human plane; they had lost a loving and protective father, and with him, a whole way of life. There was money and property enough to share between Austine, his daughter by his first marriage (which had ended disastrously in divorce very shortly after its inception) and Julie-Anne, who was his step-daughter by his second marriage, but neither of them considered money and property adequate consolation for the loss of a parent who had been more of a friend. Julie-Anne's mother had died in a car accident a year after the second marriage, when Julie-Anne was eight and Austine only two; to both of them the famous film actor who was their father had been everything, father, mother, confidant, companion, for as long as either of them could remember. He had never married again, his first two unfortunate essays into matrimony had been enough. His private life had been centred on his pretty girls, and when he died he left them well provided for, but all alone.

'It wouldn't be so awful if we had only just one close relative,' said Austine, breaking what had been a long silence. Most people would not have found her situation particularly awful, but these things are comparative. To someone who has never wanted for material things, they are very little consolation in a crisis.

'He'll have made some arrangement,' comforted Julie-Anne.

'Why should he?' asked Austine, miserably.

'There's bound to be trustees and things.'

Austine looked up, a horrified look on her face.

'You don't suppose I'll have to go to my mother, do you?'

'Don't worry,' said Julie-Anne, dispassionately. 'She's far too selfish to take you. We'll probably just stay here. I can look after us both.'

'Can you stop Mr Achenbaum trying to turn me into an actress?' asked Austine.

'I can try...' said Julie-Anne. She looked at her sister doubtfully. 'Do you really not want to be in films? Most girls seem to want to give their eye-teeth for your chances.'

'No,' said Austine. 'Look what it did for – well, for Marilyn Monroe, for instance. Or my mother.'

'Your mother did for herself,' said Julie-Anne, who had no admiration for that famous and glamorous lady. 'What would you like to do, if you could choose?'

'I'm not sure, but not acting. I don't want to be "the daughter of the brilliant star", I want to be me, on my own account. If I went on the stage, even my name isn't really my own.' She looked curiously across at Julie-Anne. 'What about you? You've never said.'

'No.' Julie-Anne looked back at her thoughtfully. 'It didn't seem necessary even to think about it. There was just life here, and it went on...plenty to do, plenty to see...plenty of money. Rather selfish, when you look back at it.'

'Don't you want to get married, or anything?'

'Not to anyone I've met so far,' said Julie-Anne, and then, sitting up suddenly, added, 'Was that a car? Oh, good heavens, he can't be here already. Hubert!'

Austine scrambled hurriedly to her feet.

'He can, you know. Look at the time! Come on, if we run we'll make it through the back door before he comes on to the terrace, and it'll give us time to change!'

The two girls fled swiftly across the lawn, but before they were half-way to the house a tall young man came out through the French doors and hailed them.

'Hi, don't run away – it's me.'

'I can see it is,' muttered Julie-Anne, and paused in her flight. Austine, too, hesitated.

'You're early,' she said, accusingly. 'We were just going in to get changed.'

'Don't bother – you look very nice as you are. It's hot, isn't it?' He gestured towards the pool. 'It looks very pleasant here- shall we discuss what we have to over a nice cold drink?'

Julie-Anne pushed her hair back from her face and held it there, looking dubious.

'It doesn't seem respectful,' she suggested, indicating Austine's brief green bikini with a gesture of her free hand. She herself, in white with daisies, looked much the same as her sister.

'Rubbish. Come and sit down.'

They followed him reluctantly over to the pool, where Austine pulled forward a chair, and Julie-Anne poured their guest a drink. Both of them still felt mildly uncomfortable; Hubert Lacey was their late father's attorney; he was here, by appointment, to discuss with them the details of their father's will, and they had planned to receive him, decently clad, in the big drawing-room indoors.

Strangely, Lacey himself seemed a little ill-at-ease also, although it obviously had nothing to do with their bizarre costume, and the unusual venue for reading a will. He fiddled with the papers in his briefcase and did not look at them. Julie-Anne slipped on her beach-wrap, in which she felt a little better, and sat down on a chair close by. Austine, who had no wrap, curled up on the warm paving slabs opposite them.

'Well?' prompted Julie-Anne, after a pause.

Lacey shuffled his papers, pulled out the will, and looked uncomfortable.

'Let me read this to you first,' he said. 'I won't go through it word for word, just give you the gist. It's very simple; one or two minor bequests, a substantial sum to various theatrical charities, and the main bulk of the property divided between you two...' His voice droned on in the summery heat, and Julie-Anne and Austine listened obediently. There were few surprises; money and property was fairly divided between the two of them, investments, stocks and shares, town and country houses, deposits abroad, all neatly parcelled out. There was a good lot of it, more, in fact, than either girl had expected, but nothing to account for Lacey's manifest uneasiness.

After a while, the lawyer's voice tailed off, almost in mid-sentence, and he looked up. He looked, Julie-Anne thought, as near as a lawyer ever comes to looking sheepish. She found herself, in spite of the solemnity of the occasion, laughing, and as she laughed she caught herself thinking that he had caught them early and informally on purpose, knowing, as he must, that Austine at least had already had about as much as she could take, and wishing to spare them just a little of the depressing ritual of death. Her heart warmed to him.

'Come on,' she said. 'Out with it. What are you trying to hide?'

'To hide?' asked Lacey, playing for time, and took a quick swig at his drink. He took a desperate plunge at the thing that embarrassed him. 'Look,' he said. 'There are one or two things that you don't realise. You see, your father knew some years ago that he was likely to die suddenly, he's had that heart condition for longer than he let anyone know except his doctor – and me. He came to me to discuss what he was going to do with you two. Five years ago, this was, and he didn't know that he would go on as long as he did. There was no natural guardian to take over if he died. Of course, there were plenty of people he could appoint as trustees, but he said... he thought...look, this is difficult, but I'm only repeating what he said, it had nothing to do with me, you do understand? I was against it...I think.'

'Of course,' said Julie-Anne. Austine, who so far had said nothing, gave a quick nod.

'Well,' said Mr Lacey, continuing, 'he said that he thought neither of you would be happy left here without him; the family unit once broken, he said, and you would both need something more out of life than sheltered luxury. And if you didn't, he wanted you to have it, anyway. If he hadn't known that he was liable to die at any time, he would have done something about you before – indeed, I advised him most strongly to tell – warn you, if you like – and to see you both with a future planned ahead, but he was afraid that you would grieve too long and suffer too much, and since he could go off at any minute, he wished to keep you both here with him until the end. It went on longer than any of us expected, which makes it difficult for me now.'

'You had better stop hedging and tell us, Hubert,' said Julie-Anne. 'What's he done? Put everything in trust for our old age and turned us penniless on the world to earn our living?'

'Good heavens no! He would never do anything like that!' The young lawyer sounded horrified. 'Everything is in trust, yes, but not for your old age.'

'What, then?' asked Julie-Anne. 'You had much better come to the point, we aren't going to blame you, you know, but the suspense is killing us.'

Hubert Lacey let his eyes dwell on her for a moment. Austine was the beauty of the family, everyone admitted that, but he personally thought Julie-Anne, although less physically beautiful, by far the more attractive; she had a liveliness and humour that coloured her personality in vivid colours. Austine, quieter, more thoughtful, to his mind was overshadowed by her half-sister. He wondered what would become of them both.

'It was this way,' he began. 'When your father learned that his heart was bad, both of you were young – Austine was twelve, you were not quite eighteen. He had seen in his time what can happen to rich young ladies with no one to keep a proper eye on them, and he wanted the utmost protection for you two. He wouldn't choose any of his friends, although I advised him to do so. He said that they were, most of them, people who would naturally see that life went on for you as it had always done, and he didn't think that you wanted that. He didn't want you to drift, and he didn't want you to fall foul of people who might take advantage of you. To a certain extent, he protected you from possible fortune-hunters by the provisions of his will; you both enjoy the interest from your legacies, but the principle is held in trust until you are twenty-four years old. He felt – and in this I agree with him – that up to that age, it was possible that love could outrun judgement. Up until that time, if you marry without the consent of the guardian he appointed, the money continues to remain in trust, either until the marriage breaks down or, failing that, it passes to any children of the marriage, the interest still remaining your income during your lifetime.'

'Suppose there are no children, but the marriage doesn't break down?' asked Julie-Anne, wrinkling up her nose in thought.

'In that case, the matter is left to the discretion of your guardian and the executors of the will – myself, and your late father's agent, Mr Achenbaum.'

Austine sat up. 'These executors haven't any say in what we do, have they?'

'We have no say in anything. We are simply there to see that there is no chance of your money being withheld due to prejudice.'

'This guardian,' said Julie-Anne, 'does he perform any other duties, besides protecting our money?'

'He agreed with your father to take on any responsibilities for you both which would normally have been those of a parent,' said Lacey. 'That is to say, until such time as you come of full age, your home is with him, if you wish it, and what you do, or wish to do, should be with his knowledge and consent. This, of course, no longer applies to you, Julie-Anne, but you still cannot marry without his consent.'

'" He",' said Julie-Anne. 'Who is he, if not one of Daddy's friends? I think there is a catch in this.'

Hubert Lacey looked uncomfortable, and both the girls came and sat beside him, one on his left, one on his right.

'Tell,' said Austine.

'Come on, we won't eat you for it,' said Julie-Anne. 'So long as it isn't Mr Achenbaum, Austine won't care, and it doesn't make that much difference to me, anyway. I've only six months to wait before I can marry my fortune-hunter.'

'Your father had some revolutionary ideas,' said Lacey, putting a companionable arm around each of them, for he had known them on a friendly basis for a long time. 'He felt that, by the time he died, you would both be of an age to resent a replacement of parental authority. He thought that whoever he appointed should be young enough to be on your side of the so-called generation gap. More of a – a brother, than a father.'

There was a long, still, silence.

'I have a brother,' said Austine, after a while. 'At least so I have always been told.'

'You have,' nodded Lacey, and then, taking the plunge, 'he's the guardian your father chose.'

'Good heavens!' exclaimed Julie-Anne, before she could stop herself. Austine drew a deep breath, and let it out again.

'Well,' she said, judicially, 'it could have been worse. It could have been poor Mr Achenbaum. You had better tell us all about it, hadn't you?'

'How much do you already know?' asked Lacey.

'Nothing at all,' said Julie-Anne.

'Just that my mother was married before she met Daddy,' said Austine. 'Twice, as a matter of fact, but the first time she had a son. It was the only time,' she went on, without bitterness, 'that she ever left a husband and took a child with her. She'd lost him somewhere along the way by the time she reached America. That's all. I don't know who his father was, or what his name was, or where she left him, or anything. I don't believe she knows much more, either, but she talks about him sometimes when she's feeling sentimental.'

'Yes, well, that sounds an admirable account of her side of the story,' said Lacey. 'I can add nothing to it. As you know, your mother, delightful as she is, is the most completely selfish person you would ever wish to meet, and that much is all she ever told anyone. However, your father met him – the son, that is – around the time that he was first taken ill, and was very impressed with him. His name is Merlin Ravenscourt, and he is twelve years your senior.'

'My mother always says that his father was the only man she ever truly loved,' remarked Austine, who had never believed a word of it. 'He was English, and his brother was a lord. Does that make this – who did you say? – a lord, too?'

'No,' said Lacey, hiding a smile. 'Just a plain Mister. His father, however, has since been knighted and is Sir Richard Ravenscourt. That makes no difference to the status of the son, however, who is still just plain Mister.'

'Never mind his father, said Julie-Anne. 'It's the son who needs to worry us. Where did Daddy meet him? He hasn't been in England for years.'

'He met him in Canada. He worked for the Forestry.'

'Canada – that's not too bad,' said Austine. 'I thought I was about to be flung across the globe.'

'Worked, the man said,' said Julie-Anne, watching Lacey. 'I believe you were right the first time.'

'I'm afraid so,' said Lacey. 'Not that it necessarily means that you'll have to go to England; that will depend largely on what you decide you want to do, and whether your brother is prepared to give it his approval. He returned to England about four years ago, and at present we are still trying to trace him.'

'Trace him?' echoed Julie-Anne. 'You mean, he's disappeared?'

'No, no. He went to live with his uncle, the then Lord Storre, in the south of England somewhere, but his uncle died a year back, and since his grandson inherited, your brother seems to have left Ravenscourt Place. His family will know where he's gone, but for the moment the matter has to be held in abeyance. We shall be able to decide what to do with you both when we hear from him.'

'Why did he take me on, as well as Austine?' asked Julie-Anne. 'I'm not his sister.'

'You're Austine's.'

'Step-sister, not even half-sister. He must be crazy, this…this…who?'

'Merlin Ravenscourt.'

'Gracious heavens!' said Julie-Anne. 'Only someone like Anabel could find a name like that!'

'Crazy or not, your father asked him to assume the charge of you both, and he agreed. I think, however, that he never expected the charge to devolve upon him. He had no idea that there was anything wrong, and he must have considered it unlikely in the extreme that he would ever be called upon to act.'

'His mistake,' said Austine. 'He may live to regret it.'

When Lacey had taken his leave and left them, promising to let them know as soon as he heard any news, the two girls stood and looked at each other.

'What do you think?' asked Austine. 'Will I have to go to England to this brother, do you think?'

'Like the man said, it depends,' said Julie-Anne. 'Would you mind?'

'Would you come with me?'

'Why not? It might be fun. Anything,' said Julie-Anne, with sudden decision, 'anything would be better than staying here, now everything has gone…no, not gone. Changed.'

'He thought it all out so carefully,' said Austine, slowly. 'He was right, you know – we'd have resented a substitute father pushing us around. He's given us – well, freedom but not complete freedom – me, at any rate, it won't make much difference to you. You'll be twenty-four almost at once. Do you think he'll want me to be an actress? Mr Achenbaum might talk him round.'

'Depends,' said Julie-Anne. 'Everything depends. On this brother of yours with the romantic name, who fells trees, or whatever, for a living. The only thing you can be sure of, if Daddy picked him out from all the people he knows – knew – as a suitable guardian for you, he's all right, whoever he is. He's your natural guardian, anyway. He's your brother.'

'Yes, but look at the parent we have in common,' said Austine, worriedly. 'Oh, Julie – ' she burst out, suddenly, I wish he hadn't died – I wish – ' She stopped, and swallowed hard. 'Oh, come on – let's have a swim.'

In the event, the tracing of the elusive guardian proved unexpectedly easy. Reading of the death of Austin Willerby in his morning paper, Merlin Ravenscourt sent an email to the executors of his will, and followed it up with a letter, also an email, which Lacey brought round to the house when he had digested its contents. Austine's half-brother had entered into a partnership with a friend, building boats for a living, it appeared, and the business was still in its infancy and could not be abandoned just like that. However, in view of the present ages of his two wards, he suggested, why didn't they both take a holiday in England in order that the whole thing could be discussed in person, as he did not feel that letters or even emails were going to be wholly satisfactory. Austine, who had half hoped that nothing more than correspondence need pass between them, was not sure that she agreed with this idea, but Hubert Lacey, backed up by his co-executor, Mr Achenbaum, thought the suggestion sound.

'What do you think?' Austine asked Julie-Anne. 'You haven't said anything.'

'Well, it doesn't concern me that much,' said Julie-Anne. 'I do think, though, that considering you know nothing about him, and that for the next few years you are rather in his hands, it would be silly to antagonize him right at the start. I don't want to sound pessimistic, but after all, the only thing you know about him is that he's your mother's son, and you know what she can be like.'

'You said that Daddy wouldn't have chosen him if he hadn't been all right,' said Austine, accusingly.

'I know I did, and I still believe it, but there's two sides to everything. You must allow for a little human nature. Don't get all hot and bothered about it-if you go, I'm coming too, and even when I'm the magic age of twenty-four, I shan't just run out on you. I'll stick around. But I think we should go. You've got seven years of your sentence still to run, and if he doesn't know you, or you him, they're going to be unnecessarily hard, don't you think? And there's nothing stopping us. Speaking for myself, I'd like to get away.'

'So would I, but...'

'I tell you what,' said Julie-Anne, seeing her still hesitating and, indeed, understanding that hesitation. 'We'll write to him – not just an email, a proper letter, it'll be more personal. We'll bypass Hubert and Mr Achenbaum, and we'll write to him ourselves. He's our guardian, we've got a perfect right. Will it make you feel any better if we do that?'

'It might be a bit better,' admitted Austine. 'It's this awful impersonality that I hate. You'd think he didn't care about us. Just "I can't get away, so they'll have to come here." Like luggage.'

'Baggages, more like,' said Julie-Anne. 'How old is this Merlin? Twenty-eight? Twenty-nine? Young enough for us to give him a pretty good run for his money, anyway. You wait, Tina, if he gets stuffy on us, we'll show him who's boss! We'll big brother him! He'll be sorry he ever opened his mouth if he gives us any trouble.' She paused. 'But, anyway, perhaps we won't have to. He may even turn out to be a human being. It's probably just this British reserve we hear so much about. Where's some notepaper?'

'He's Canadian,' Austine muttered, but the letter was duly written. It took some time, and, when finished, was nearly as stuffy as their guardian's letter to Lacey, but it had to do. They posted it off, and waited somewhat dubiously for the reply. In the meantime, in order to give Austine courage, Julie-Anne collected travel brochures on the British Isles and tried to think of as many good points that Merlin Ravenscourt could have inherited from his mother as possible. They weren't too numerous, but the worst fault, as she pointed out, must have by-passed him. If he had inherited her selfishness, he would never have agreed to the guardianship in the first place.

The lady whom Austine always referred to as 'my mother' in conversation but who like to be called 'Anabel' to her face, was still in the background of their lives. They did not see her often; young girls, particularly when they were as beautiful as her daughter, did not appeal to Anabel Findlater. She herself possessed fame, charm, beauty, and wealth, and flitted from man to man as promiscuously as the family cat. She was completely selfish; she was also extremely shrewd. Having long since discovered that marriage for love was uncomfortable, she had since married only for further fame or money, and had done very well on the strength of it. She had a great deal of surface warmth, which deceived people into thinking that she was genuinely concerned about them, and by the time that they had learned differently, they were usually so much under her spell that they forgave her anything. Of her five marriages to date, only two had produced any children: of those, she had abandoned one as a baby, leaving her with her father and passing on herself to the next husband. That was Austine, and she was the luckier of the two. The first child, the son born to that unhappy love-match that the young Anabel had made on the threshold of her turbulent career, had been less fortunate. When she left her first husband, Anabel had taken the boy with her. She had very soon discovered that toting a small child around with her was a bore, and had gradually eased the burden on to the shoulders of anybody who would accept it. Merlin Ravenscourt, reared in a series of foster homes and boarding schools, and finally left to find his own salvation, could have turned into almost anything. Both Austine and Julie-Anne were well aware of it, and although Julie-Anne, almost clear of his guardianship, repeatedly urged her step-sister to trust their late father's judgement, Austine was constantly haunted by the fact that she could well find herself in the hands of someone who had at least some of her mother's less attractive traits. Her father, indeed, could have fallen a victim to that same charm with which Anabel had snared him when she wished for his reputation as a stepping-stone for her own. The difference being, as Julie-Anne had pointed out, that Anabel would never have taken on the responsibility of anyone else's children; she could not even be bothered with her own.

The letter eventually arrived. It sat on the breakfast table, addressed in an unfamiliar hand to Miss A. Willerby and Miss J. Austin. Neither of the girls seemed in a hurry to open it.

'Nice handwriting,' said Julie-Anne, making no attempt to pick it up.

'Hmm,' said Austine, through a mouthful of toast. She swallowed, and said, more clearly, 'Untidy.'

'Yes, but nice with it.'

'Well,' said Austine, after a pause, 'read it, then.'

'Don't you want to?'

'You're the eldest.'

'He's your brother.'

'Oh, come on,' said Austine, reaching for the letter. 'He can't bite us in a letter?' She slit it open, unfolded it, and paused again, knitting her brows. 'I can't,' she said.

'Can't what?'

'Read it. I didn't study Sanskrit at High School. Look.' She tossed the frail sheet across the breakfast table, and Julie-Anne picked it up.

'Oh…I see what you mean. Yes. Well, the address is clear enough.'

'It's a rubber stamp,' said Austine.

"Ravenscourt Place, Shearwater, Dorset." That must be the family seat. *Dear Austine and smear-Anne* – I say, do you think he'd take it as an insult if we sent him a new pen? I think that's half his trouble.'

'Go on,' commanded Austine.

'*Thank you for writing, I was placed* – placed? – no, *pleased to hear from you both, as I was… was wearying?*"

'Worrying?'

'Could be. *Worrying about how you would react to your father's plans for you. I was very sorry to hear of his death, and please accept my sympathy for you both. He was a fine man. I met him two or three times, and he impressed me with his great affection for you both. I expect you miss him a great deal.* He can say that again. *I understand from your father's lawyer, Mr Lacey, that he never told you what he intended, and your letter bears this out. I'm sorry, because it doesn't make things any easier for us all. He didn't…*didn't…I think he means "intend", but I'm not certain. *He didn't intend that I should be anything more than someone in the background whom you could turn to if you needed. Both of you are old enough to know your own minds. I'm simply here to help you with the mechanics of it all and to give you a base if you need one. Of course, when he made this arrangement I was in Canada, which was more handy, but circumstances brought me back to England, and for a while, at least, they're going to keep me here. I'd come over if I could, but as I can't at present, I suggested to Mr Lacey that you might like to see a bit of the world and take me in on the way. He tells me neither of you had any job to worry about, and they do say that…*What's he on about?'

'I don't know, unless you tell me,' said Austine.

'Well, it looks like, foreign travel broadens the mind. I suppose it could be.'

'Sounds like Daddy,' commented Austine. 'That's the sort of thing he used to say. Go on.'

'He doesn't say much else. *You don't have to stay over here, as far as I'm concerned your lives have to be your own, but since we are, legally at least, bound to each other it will be far easier, don't you agree, if we have met each other. Of course, if you want to stay, that's another thing altogether. You can count on me, in any case, for practical assistance, and I hope I may look forward to meeting you both in the near future. Let me know what you decide to do, and when you decide to do it. Yours sincerely, Merlin Ravenscourt.* Umm. Well, that at least sounds as if he isn't meaning to throw his weight about.'

'We might as well go – mightn't we?'

'Yes, why not? We can spend Christmas abroad somewhere and go on to England in the New Year...I don't want to spend Christmas here. Not this year.'

'Nor me.'

'We'll do that, then. Christmas in Austria, or somewhere where there's snow. Then England. I don't think January is the best time for England, but it wouldn't be polite to leave it any later. We'll ask Mr Achenbaum what he thinks.'

'Much better ask Hubert,' said Austine.

Julie-Anne grinned. 'Has he been on to you again?'

'Waving contracts,' said Austine. 'He knows I can't act – look at that awful film I made when I was fourteen.'

'Yes, but you're the only person who thinks it was awful,' said Julie-Anne. 'And you're a name. He's bound to want you under contract – Austine Willerby, daughter of the great Austin Willerby. It sounds good. Still, Daddy said you could make up your own mind, and this Merlin doesn't sound as if he minds much either way. We're agreed that we're off to England?'

'I suppose so...' said Austine.

II

'Down with Big Brother.'
George Orwell: Nineteen Eighty-Four

Arrangements for the trip to England went ahead. The plan that Julie-Anne and Austine made was that they would sail to Europe, spend a fortnight over the Christmas period in Salzburg, and then fly on to London, and from thence make their way down to Dorset by train. By the time other people had added their embellishments, although basically the same, it had a rather different general appearance. They met with a surprising amount of opposition, for one thing, to their travelling alone.

'Too rich, and too beautiful,' said Mr Achenbaum, who had known them both for years and loved them both like daughters and who would, indeed, have liked to have them in his care and that of his smart but kind-hearted wife. 'Also, too young and too inexperienced. You've never travelled alone.'

'You'd be dreadfully lonely, my dears,' said Mrs Achenbaum. 'Over Christmas, too, which has always been such a family time for you all.'

'I don't think it's advisable,' said Hubert. 'Someone must travel with you.'

'Who?' asked Julie-Anne, warily.

'We'll find someone,' said Lacey'

In the end, it was Mr and Mrs Achenbaum.

'The least we can do for poor Austin's kids,' said Mr Achenbaum.

'I've always adored Austria, and the Austrians really do Christmas well,' said Mrs Achenbaum.

Austine and Julie-Anne were unable to feel properly appreciative, but said thank you and very little else. Mr and Mrs Achenbaum were to put them on an aeroplane at Salzburg, and from thence they were to fly to England, and then go on to Dorset by train. Even more surprising interference in this plan came from their unknown guardian, who wrote and said that Shearwater was at the back of beyond, and rather than have them shuffling round the southern counties on a railway train, he would meet them himself at Heathrow and drive them down to Ravenscourt Place.

'Fine adventurous time we're going to have,' said Austine. 'Two hours or something, fantastic freedom on an aeroplane! I dare say Mr Achenbaum will ask the stewardess to take special care of us.'

'You should feel cherished,' said Julie-Anne.

'Well, I don't. I feel stifled. We're quite old enough to take care of ourselves.

'We've led very sheltered lives,' said Julie-Anne, dulcetly.

'We're going to go on living them, aren't we?' said Austine. 'At this rate, we'll still be sheltered when we're in our nineties.'

'By that time it'll be difficult to find an older person to chaperon us,' Julie-Anne offered.

'Huh!'

'Be thankful,' said Julie-Anne. 'At one time, Mr and Mrs Achenbaum were going to London with us, to make sure we were safely handed over.'

'Oh no!'

'Oh yes. So count your blessings. I did at least talk them out of that one.'

In the event, this turned out to be lucky. Had Mr and Mrs Achenbaum flown to Heathrow with the girls, events might have taken a rather different course. As it was, everything, up to a point, went like clockwork; they sailed from New York on the 15th of December, and were in Salzburg by Christmas Eve. Christmas was lovely, so different from anything that Austine and Julie-Anne had ever experienced that they were able to ignore, in the main, the horrid dull ache that came when they thought of Christmases past. Austine only once asked,

'Where will we by next Christmas, do you think?' And Julie-Anne, to cover the moment, replied, 'Here again, I hope. I've never had such a time. I—' She broke off, and did not add, as she had started to say, 'I wish we had come here with Daddy.'

They stayed in Austria over the New Year, and had the time of their lives. On the 2nd of January, Mr and Mrs Achenbaum kissed them goodbye and abandoned them to the care of the Austrian Airline.

'Be sure and write to let us know how you get on,' said Mr Achenbaum. 'Don't get so fond of England you don't come back home again.'

'Be careful,' said Mrs Achenbaum. 'I'm sure this brother will take good care of you, but come back safely in the spring. We'll miss you.'

The Achenbaums waited until the plane had safely taken off, before making their way back to the hotel.

'Lovely girls,' said Mr Achenbaum. 'That Austine – I could have done with her. Oh, well, they'll be back in the spring.'

'Will they?' said Mrs Achenbaum. 'I wonder. I've got a feeling…'

'You and your feelings,' said Mr Achenbaum, and did not tell her that he, too, had a feeling that Julie-Anne and Austine would not readily return to the United States. He merely said, almost to himself, 'Well, if she decided to stay, I can find some good contacts for her over there.'

'I only hope Austin knew what he was doing,' said Mrs Achenbaum, and swallowed a strange lump in her throat. 'So far away…'

'Oh, come on, love, cheer up. Let's go have a drink.'

High overhead, the aeroplane carrying Austin Willerby's beloved girls flew on towards England.

★★★

The plane landed safely in the early afternoon, after an uneventful flight, and the passengers disembarked and were shepherded through Customs. Julie-Anne and Austine, conscious for the first time of a slight sinking feeling, began to wonder.

'How will we know him?' asked Austine.

'He'll know us,' suggested Julie-Anne. 'Two beautiful young girls…I wonder if he's like Anabel. To look at, I mean. I wouldn't mind a really dishy guardian. Would you?'

'He's my brother,' Austine reminded her. 'It's no skin off my nose. Do you think he will know us? Perhaps we should have worn a white gardenia, or something.'

They were disgorged into the Arrival Hall, and stood among their suitcases, looking round them. Nobody remotely like their idea of a guardian seemed to be there, but after a while Julie-Anne became conscious that she was being watched. She turned her head a little and found that a tall, dark and handsome young man was looking at her steadily from a chair on the far side of the room. He raised an eyebrow at her, ran his eye over Austine's unconscious back, and got to his feet.

'Hello,' said Julie-Anne, 'I think we've just been found.'

Austine turned round just as the young man reached them. He was, on closer inspection, extremely handsome, dark haired, with cool grey eyes fringed with thick black lashes and a most engaging smile, but he didn't look old enough to be anybody's guardian.

'Hello,' he said, with a touch of diffidence that was somehow charming. 'Are you, by any chance, Julie-Anne and Austine? I hardly liked to believe it, but I can't see any other unclaimed young women.'

'That's us,' said Julie-Anne. 'Are you…are you Merlin?' She spoke hesitantly, because he was so different from what she had expected.

'Well, no, actually,' said the young man. 'I'm Sylvester – his cousin. There's been a slight technical hitch, I'm afraid. Look here, it's early for lunch, but there's two hours before I have to put you on a train, so shall I explain over a pot of tea, or something?'

'Thank you,' said Julie-Anne. 'That would be nice, wouldn't it, Austine?'

'Lovely,' said Austine. 'I say, what a good thing Mr Achenbaum didn't come. What's gone wrong?'

'You might well ask,' said Sylvester. 'If you knew my cousin Merlin, come to that, you wouldn't even bother to ask. Whatever your parent was thinking of, to leave you in the care of such a lunatic, I can't imagine. Nice with it, of course,' he went on, stacking their suitcases in a corner with skill and efficiency, 'but mad as a March hare.' He took them each by an arm and shepherded them towards the restaurant. 'Come on, tea and cakes and explanations, and then I'll drive you to the station.'

'Do you live in London, then?' asked Austine, idly, as they found a table.

'Me? No. I live with my nephew, Robin, and my cousin, of whom you know, at the family ancestral home. I've got to be back there tonight to be at work in the morning, or I'd take you to a show and put you on a later train. Pity. I expect you know how decorative you both are. Tea? Sandwiches? What?'

'Where,' asked Julie-Anne, looking at him steadily, 'where is this train of ours going to?'

'Lowestoft. Suffolk. Change at Ipswich. I'll explain to you in a moment.' He floated off in search of tea, and Austine and Julie-Anne looked at each other.

'Suffolk? Suffolk? Where's Suffolk?' asked Julie-Anne.

'Quiet and sheltered and unadventurous,' said Austine, with satisfaction. 'This travel business is at last beginning to do its job and broaden the mind. I don't know where Suffolk is, but we shall find out soon. Rather more to the point, at the moment, where's my brother?'

'He'll tell us when he comes back,' said Julie-Anne, with a gesture towards Sylvester. 'If that's the Ravenscourt side of the family, mixed with Anabel, it should be quite something. I'm beginning to enjoy this expedition.'

'He's probably as plain as a pikestaff,' said Austine, with a grin.

'Rubbish, no son of Anabel's would be as plain as a pikestaff. He wouldn't dare,' said Julie-Anne.

'Of course,' said Austine, wrinkling up her nose, 'we never asked, and he never said, but he could be married.'

'True. Oh well, there's always this cousin to brighten the days. Something will have to – just look at the weather out there!'

'It's raining,' agreed Austine. 'It does, in England, so I'm told, particularly in January.'

Sylvester returned with a tray of tea and sandwiches, and sat down with them. 'Now then,' he said. 'What shall I tell you first?'

'Where's Suffolk?' asked Austine.

'Suffolk? Oh...up on the east coast. Why?'

'Nothing, only we thought we were going to Dorset?'

'So you were. So you are. Only you're making a slight detour. It's Merlin's fault. You see, he went up to see his father – he does every so often, it's a sort of duty call. I don't believe either of them enjoys it much, but a father is a father when all's said and done. His father lives in Suffolk.'

'What kept him?' asked Julie-Anne.

'Ah, you're beginning to grasp the plot, I see. Yes, well...He should have been back two days ago, but he fell in the drain on a rather chilly night, and – '

'He did what?' asked Austine, disbelievingly.

'Fell in the drain. It's a sort of – oh, you'll see when you get there. Like an irrigation ditch, only bigger, and not for irrigation. As I said, it was cold, and he phoned up yesterday in a bit of a state, and said he wasn't fit to travel, so I said I'd get the day off, but what was I to do with you, and he said –'

'Put us on a train for Lowestoft, Suffolk. Change at Ipswich,' nodded Julie-Anne.

'That's it. So I'm going to.'

'What happens when we get to Lowestoft, Suffolk?' enquired Austine.

'Well, I'm not certain, for that part of it hardly concerns me – I shall be in Shearwater, Dorset. I assume that my Uncle Richard's aged retainer with meet you and convey you to Raven's Dyke – which is another family seat, by the way – and when Merlin has recovered from whatever it is that ails him, you'll come and join me and Robin at Ravenscourt Place. The sooner the better, and I don't say that only for my sake. Yours too.'

'Ours too?'

'Wait until you see Raven's Dyke, said Sylvester. 'You'll see what I mean.'

'Supposing we're not met?' asked Julie-Anne. 'Where is this Raven's Dyke? Can we get a taxi?'

'A taxi?' Sylvester looked blank. 'I suppose so – it's a long way though, it'd cost a bomb. Better get a bus. It's at a place called Whytham St Giles, but I'm sure you'll be met. If Merlin had enough of a grip on the situation to telephone me, he'll remember that bit I expect.'

'What's the matter with him?' asked Austine.

'He said he'd caught a chill. On the telephone it sounded like double pneumonia. Don't worry about him, he's good, healthy stock. It's just that iced drains aren't the best place to take a bath in midwinter, particularly on the east coast. It'll teach him to stay sober in future.'

'Wasn't he sober?' asked Austine.

'He says he was, but good grief, nobody in their senses goes swimming in a drain in January. He'd been down to the Lamb and Flag – Raven's Dyke would drive anyone to drink.'

'Or drains,' said Austine.

'It's more fun at Ravenscourt Place,' Sylvester comforted them. 'The trouble with Whytham St Giles is that nobody lives there. It's the original land that God forgot. The southlands are friendlier. You'll like it in Shearwater.'

'But not in Whytham St where-did-you-say? I hope your cousin recovers quickly,' observed Julie-Anne.

'He will. If he doesn't, I'll come up at the weekend and cheer you up, I promise. You'll need something by then – '

'Look, stop harping on the dreariness of the place, do you mind?' asked Julie-Anne amused. 'What are you trying to do? Make us cry? I warn you, we're hardier than that.'

'I wouldn't dream of it, said Sylvester. 'I just thought you should be warned.' He smiled, a sudden flashing smile that would have turned the heart over in any red-blooded woman. 'I must say, I hope you come home soon. And I'm really sorry to be missing Merlin's first reaction to you. To say that he was shattered when your father died would be to put it mildly.'

There was a sudden silence.

'Didn't he want to be bothered with us, then?' said Austine, in a small voice.

'Oh, no, no, no. I've said the wrong thing, haven't I? I'm sorry. No, it wasn't like that. It's just that I think he'd almost forgotten the arrangement, and it came as rather a shock. He got used to it. It's his girlfriend who got really mad.'

'I'm sorry,' said Julie-Anne.

'Don't worry about it,' repeated Sylvester. 'It's nothing, it just slipped out. These things happen. Merlin'll get over it if she stays up in the air.'

'All this, and drains too,' said Julie-Anne. 'We seem to have disrupted his life pretty thoroughly already.'

'You can't disrupt a life that stays in a permanent state of disruption,' said Sylvester. 'I told you – he's crazy, anyway. The whole family is, when you think about it. Look at me.'

'We're looking,' said Austine.

'Yes, well, there's no need to look in that tone of voice, my child. Finished? Then if you don't want any more tea, let's go find ourselves a railway station.'

Sylvester rattled on cheerfully as they drove across London, asking questions, providing information about the places along the route, making plans for when they should meet again in Dorset. Julie-Anne thought that he was talking hard to cover his social slip-up, and for the first time found herself wondering exactly what Austine's half-brother thought about it all. They had assumed, since he had agreed to the arrangement, that he was content with it, but in six years, of course, a lot of things could have changed for him. The one thing that had never occurred to either herself or Austine was that Merlin would be as reluctant about the whole thing as they were. It was a new thought, and a disquieting one, and she kept it to herself for Austine, sitting in the front of the car beside Sylvester, was greatly enjoying herself and obviously had no such thoughts in her head. Julie-Anne decided that she was not going to put them there. Austine had seven years to go under this reluctant guardianship, and things had a way of working themselves out if they were given enough time. Not caring one way or the other was the one thing, active resentment could prove quite another. On the other hand, Sylvester, though charming, was hardly the soul of discretion, and Julie-Anne had already noticed that he had a keen sense of mischief.

Their train was already in when they arrived at Liverpool Street, and Sylvester, having found them two corner seats and stowed their luggage for them, prepared to take his departure.

'I'll be up at the weekend, if you're not home by then,' he promised, as he left. 'Don't let the place get you down. Nowhere's at its best in January. Have a good journey.'

'Goodbye,' called Austine, after his retreating back. He turned and waved, and the two girls sat down and looked at each other.

'He's nice, said Austine. 'Don't you think so?'

'I thought he was delightful,' said Julie-Anne, honestly, 'but he makes me feel like Grandma.'

'I'm beginning to feel better about England,' said Austine. She reached for the magazine that Sylvester had bought her, and eyed her sister consideringly. 'How about you?' she asked.

'Me?'

'Yes. Are you enjoying it? It's more of an adventure than we expected, isn't it?'

'Oh – adventure! I just hope that when we get to this Raven's Dyke place they have central heating – but I have a horrible feeling that they won't.'

'I shouldn't think so,' said Austine, gaily, 'but at least they've got drains...'

At Ipswich, the rain, which had been falling steadily since they landed at Heathrow, began to turn to sleet, and the temperature was noticeably lower. The sky was dark above them, and Austine's high spirits, induced by the interval in Sylvester's company, began to fall a little. By the time their train drew in to Lowestoft both she and Julie-Anne were feeling more sympathetic towards a guardian who did not want them 'shuffling round the southern counties on a railway train.' They had both of them had enough of shuffling round the eastern counties.

At Lowestoft there was no friendly, cheerful Sylvester to meet them. There was an elderly man with a huge black car like a hearse, who spoke in monosyllables and seemed unfriendly, and there was a biting wind with more snow than sleet in it, and what felt like miles and miles and miles of bleak, flat, watery countryside lying between them and the hope of a warm house and a hot meal. Julie-Anne and Austine sat in the back of the hearse without speaking, looking out of the windows at the slowly darkening marshland, in which they could find nothing to admire, and their hearts sank lower and lower.

After what felt like hours, the air began to have a salty tang, as if the sea was not far off, and the car began to slow down. A tumble-down wrought-iron gate appeared on the right, and their silent driver turned between the posts and drove through a damp and dripping shrubbery to pull up in front of the first house that they had seen for miles; an old half-timbered manor house of venerable antiquity surrounded with an indefinable air of decay. Over to the right, a gleam of water showed through the shrubs; to the left a row of outbuildings sagged drearily under the weight of their years.

'Pow!' said Julie-Anne, standing on the doorstep and looking around her, 'Wuthering Heights!'

'Wuthering Depths,' muttered Austine, beside her. 'Do we ring the bell, do you think, or will he let us in?'

'Just look at the bell,' said Julie-Anne. 'Did you ever see anything like it?' It hung like an iron cow's tail beside the heavy, studded door. It was dusty. Austine said nothing.

The elderly man, laden with suitcases, came round the back of the car and, with some difficulty, opened the front door. The girls followed him inside. They found themselves in a large, dark, stone-flagged hall, with an inadequate fire spluttering and smoking in a huge fireplace. The only furniture was an enormous polished oak table in the middle of the floor, on which lay a pair of gloves, a newspaper, and a dog lead. Great beams in the ceiling added to the general air of aged decrepitude. Everywhere was spotlessly clean, shabby, and cold. Austine shivered.

The elderly chauffeur, without saying anything, disappeared in the shadows at the rear of the hall, their suitcases with him. Simultaneously, a door opened to the left of the hall, and a man appeared. Like the first occupant of Raven's Dyke that they had met, he was elderly, with a preoccupied air that made Julie-Anne and Austine feel like an unwelcome interruption, but he had a gentle courtesy about him that appeared to be doing its best to make the best of things. The same grey, black-lashed eyes that had laughed at them from Sylvester's face stared absently over their heads, but at least the words he spoke were of welcome.

'Good evening,' said Sir Richard Ravenscourt. 'So here you are! I trust that you had a good journey?'

'Not too bad, thank you,' said Julie-Anne. 'I– '

'Good, good. I expect you're tired. Mrs Bartle will show you your room and you can rest before dinner. I'm afraid that we are very old-fashioned here, but we have done our best to make you comfortable.' He smiled vaguely, and the conversation petered out. Austine and Julie-Anne, bereft of speech for once, stood beside the uncomforting fire and Sir Richard lingered absentmindedly by the table, obviously ill-at-ease and wishing to disappear back into whatever fastness he had originally left. It was a relief to all three of them when footsteps were heard coming along the stone floored passage, and a small, neat, elderly woman appeared.

'Ah, Mrs Bartle, here are Mr Merlin's young ladies,' said Sir Richard, and bolted into his hole like a startled rabbit. The door shut smartly behind him, and Mrs Bartle smiled at the girls.

'There now, we were wondering what had happened to you,' she said. 'I expect you're tired. Bartle's taken your cases up. I'll just show you to your room now and you can have a little rest before dinner. This way.'

They followed her up a dark oak staircase of great beauty, and along a low-ceilinged passage with heavy oak doors at intervals until, after going up and down several unexpected little stairs, they turned a corner and found themselves actually going through one of the many doors.

'Here you are, my dears,' said Mrs Bartle. 'I put you in here because it's near to a bathroom. I hope you don't mind sharing the bed, so few of the rooms are furnished now. If you need anything, just pull the bell. The bathroom is just down the passage on the left, I've left the door ajar. Now, if you'll excuse me, I'll go back to my kitchen. Sir Richard does like his dinner on time, so come down when you hear the gong, won't you? So inconvenient for everyone, but never mind, we'll manage…'

'Do you think she meant us…?' asked Austine, when Mrs Bartle had gone.

'I'm sure she did,' said Julie-Anne. She looked about her in awe. 'Good gracious, Tina, this is the sort of place we Americans pay small fortunes to stay in – and we're getting it for free. Just look at that bed!'

The room was large, oak panelled, with latticed windows. Another huge fireplace housed a fire, brighter and more adequate than the one downstairs, and its light flickered on heavy, dark, polished furniture, a polished wooden floor, and a huge half-tester hung with faded chintz. Julie-Anne sat down on the foot of the last-named item, and Austine sat down on an oak chest in the window.

'It isn't very warm,' she said.

'It isn't very welcoming,' said Julie-Anne. 'I get the distinct impression that we're upsetting Sir Richard's routine, only he's too much the gentleman to say so. Oh well, at least we have each other.' She began to laugh. 'What would Mr Achenbaum say if he could see us now?'

'You must be tired, have a little rest before dinner,' suggested Austine. 'Are you tired?'

'A bit. Not little-rest tired. Sitting-too-long-in-a-train-tired. Depressed tired. Not tired tired.' She got to her feet. 'I'm going exploring for the bathroom. I need a wash. Where's my dressing-case?'

Left alone, Austine leaned her chin on her hands and gave way to despair. A tear slid silently down her nose, and a wave of home-sickness engulfed her. Even Mr Achenbaum's contract didn't look so bad from the vantage point of an antique chest in an antique bedroom in an extremely antique English manor house. With a crowd of cheerless antique elderly people for company, too. Julie-Anne, returning some while later from her expedition into the depths of the bathroom came into the bedroom with laughter bubbling out of her and found her sister flung face downwards on the bed, crying her eyes out.

'Hey – Tina! What's the matter?' Julie-Anne sat down on the bed beside her and shook her shoulder. 'Don't cry, darling – what's the matter?'

'Everything!' sobbed Austine, comprehensively. 'This beastly country. This beastly house. My beastly brother. Everything.'

'I see,' said Julie-Anne. 'Come on, cheer up. It isn't really that bad. You're just tired.'

'I'm not, I'm not!' said Austine, sitting up and scrubbing at her face with a handkerchief. 'I just want to be h-h-home!'

Julie-Anne put her arms round her.

'I know, I know. It's all a bit gloomy, and it's cold, and the weather's foul, and it's a long way from anything we've experienced. But, you know, you did want a change.'

'N-n-not this sort.'

Julie-Anne gave her an affectionate shake.

'Any minute now, you'll be pining for Mr Achenbaum.'

'I was!' wailed Austine, and burst into tears again. Julie-Anne couldn't help herself. She began to laugh. After a minute Austine joined her, with a reluctant giggle.

'That's better,' said Julie-Anne. 'Go to the bathroom and have a wash and a good laugh and – '

'A good laugh?'

'You haven't seen it,' said Julie-Anne, and grinned. 'A huge mahogany throne raised up on a dais, with a beautiful willow-pattern bowl and a handle like a stirrup-pump you pull up to flush it. And the bath defies description! It's huge, and glassed in like a greenhouse. And you could hold a dance on the floor! But the water's hot, and there's clean towels.'

Austine slipped off the bed and began to look for her washing things. She sounded a little more cheerful, but reluctantly so.

'Have you looked out of the window?'

'No – should I?'

Austine said nothing, and Julie-Anne knelt on the oak chest and peered out into the fast-gathering dusk. She had a shock. The window was suspended in space, as it were, over water which gleamed dully in the fading light.

'Hey – where's the house? said Julie-Anne.

'Down there somewhere,' said Austine, who, after her outburst, was feeling a bit better. 'You know what this is? It's a moated grange! I knew there was something about it – .' She left the room, and Julie-Anne, after another startled look outside, drew the curtains against the weather and began to unpack. By the time Austine, returned, she had found a change of clothes for both of them, and laid the garments on the great bed, and was sitting in front of the dressing-table mirror brushing her hair. Her reflection looked back at her dimly in the light given by one bedside lamp – there was no overhead light. Shadowed blue eyes to a face pale with weariness from travelling, smooth, honey coloured hair just touching her shoulders, a snub nose with freckles on it. Wholesome, reflected Julie-Anne, dispassionately, the picture of healthy all-American girlhood, but it would be nice to have Austine's straight, coppery hair and unusual green eyes, her face like a Madonna, her lovely voice, and long, elegant limbs…

25

'I see what you mean about the bathroom,' said Austine's voice, in her ear. Julie-Anne jumped, and turned round.

'I never heard you come. Look, I've dug out some warm clothes – and if Sir Richard doesn't like his ladies in pants, he'll have to make the fire up a bit higher. Let's get dressed and explore.'

'Explore where?'

'Well, not the great outdoors – although I shall have to soon, to find out where the house has gone to, it fascinates me. Do you think it's really a moat?'

'Perhaps it's the famous drain,' said Austine, pulling a warm sweater over her head. 'Where then?'

'Well,' said Julie-Anne, 'somewhere in this mausoleum of a house, we have a guardian with a chill. I think it's time he did some guarding, so let's find him.'

Austine's face, with a questioning look on it, appeared through the neck of her sweater. 'How? We can't just go round the place shouting "Hi, where are you?"'

'Why not? But actually, knocking at doors was more what I had in mind. Nobody's up here but us, and him. We're bound to find him sooner or later.'

'Well, yes,' said Austine, doubtfully.

'I think it's pretty cool that he hasn't sent us any message, anyway,' said Julie-Anne. 'Not so much as "welcome". It wouldn't have hurt him.'

'Austine reached for her coat.

'If we are going along those draughty corridors, I'm taking this,' she said. 'It was warmer in the snow at Christmas. All right then, are you ready?'

'Yes, come on,' said Julie-Anne, and opened the door.

They stepped out on to the dark passage, Austin Willerby's two cherished daughters, who had led such a protected and sheltered life, and innocently and lightheartedly set out on their search for nightmare.

III

'O Lord, methought what pain it was to drown,
What dreadful noise of waters in my ears,
What signs of ugly death within my eyes!'
　　　　　　　　　　　Shakespeare: Richard III

The last of the daylight had faded from the windows and the night was wet and overcast. The passage was dark, and the old house quiet.

'It's creepy,' whispered Austine.

'Really Gothic,' whispered back Julie-Anne. 'Mind the step – 'A stumbling thud behind her told her that her warning had come too late.

'I can't see,' said Austine, urgently. 'Isn't there a light?'

'Where? Wait until we get to the stairs, there might be one there.'

'Mrs Bartle could have left it on for us.'

'They're not used to visitors.'

'You can say that again!'

They reached the head of the stairs and in the dim light from the landing window managed to find a light switch.

'Economical, too,' remarked Julie-Anne, looking up at the dim light-bulb unfavourably. 'Do you think they like it like this, or just don't notice? Which way shall we go?'

'Well, we came along there – I say, do you think we shall be able to find our way back? All those little stairs.'

'We'll hope so. This house is huge. Let's go along this way.'

'You haven't knocked at any doors.'

'I don't quite like to. It's all so quiet.'

'You can hear the rain coming down.'

'Ugh!'

They stood hesitating at the top of the stairs, and the velvet stillness gathered round them. A soft gurgling of water in the gutters and the sound of their own breathing was all that they could hear. The stairwell yawned darkly beside them.

'If this was a Gothic novel,' said Julie-Anne, still in a whisper, 'this is the moment we'd hear an awful scream – '

The words were hardly out of her mouth when it came. Not a scream – a strangled cry, bitten off short. A faint echo came from Austine, and Julie-Anne caught her breath.

'What was that?'

'Sssh – what was *that?*'

'Somebody coughing,' said Julie-Anne, prosaically. 'This way – come on.'

Austine hung back. 'That was the way where – '

'Come on!'

Julie-Anne, with Austine treading close on her heels, headed down the passage opposite to the one along which their own room lay. At the first door, she stopped.

'Knock – ' hissed Austine (as well as a word like 'knock' can be hissed, that is). Julie-Anne raised a nervous hand, but as she went to knock on the door, it moved away from her and slowly creaked open, revealing a restricted view of a lamplit room beyond.

There was a silence, worse that all the rest. And through it, over the gurgling in the gutters and the thud of their own hearts, Austine and Julie-Anne became aware of somebody breathing, not normally, but as if they had been running a race, every breath a harsh, whistling effort. There was only one thing for it – apart from flight, that is. Julie-Anne seized Austine's hand, partly for moral support, partly to make sure her ally stayed with her, and stepped forward into the room.

It was a room as big as their own, and as dark, dominated by a four-poster bed even more impressive than the half-tester. There was someone on the bed, half-sitting, half-lying, and although with the lamp behind him they could not see his face, his attitude, indeed, the feel of the whole room, spelled unbearable tension. Julie-Anne gave the door a push to close it, and dragged Austine willy-nilly into the light. The man on the great bed let out a sigh when he saw them, which turned into another coughing fit, through which he just managed to say:

'Do you mind – you nearly gave me heart failure!'

'Us too,' said Austine, whose knees were wobbling.

'Hello,' said Julie-Anne, who could think of nothing else for the moment.

He lay back, and the lamplight, from being directly behind his head, fell across his face so that for the first time they saw him properly. The same cool, grey eyes, the same black lashes, as Sir Richard and Sylvester, but there the resemblance ended. Anabel Findlater's fair skin, the same fair hair; in many ways, Anabel's face feature for feature, but in Anabel's son her beauty had been transposed into something more everyday and friendly. Nice looking, but no more. The flame that was Anabel had not been lost, but altered, when mixed with the ancient lineage of the Ravenscourts. The result should have been pleasing, and would have been, but the remnants of remembered horror still lingered in the grey eyes, heavy and lustrous with fever. Whatever had made Merlin Ravenscourt cry out was still with him.

Austine was the first one of the three to pull herself together. 'Your fire's going out,' she said, and took practical steps to deal with the situation. Julie-Anne left her to it, and walked round the bed until she stood in the pool of light cast by the lamp.

'Hello,' she said again. 'I'm Julie-Anne, she's Austine. You must be Merlin. That's a nasty cough you've got; have you seen a doctor?'

'Don't be silly,' said Austine, before Merlin could answer. 'You could die in this place, and they'd have an effort to remember to call the undertaker.'

'As bad as that?' asked Merlin. 'I'm sorry about that – I – '

'Fell in the drain,' said Julie-Anne. 'We heard. You're ill.'

'I thought that, too,' agreed Merlin. He was beginning to come back from whatever terror had held him and was looking more normal. Julie-Anne, relieved, sat down on the edge of the bed.

'You yelled,' she said. 'We were on the top of the stairs, we nearly died of shock. You sounded as if the fiends of hell were after you.'

'In a way, they were,' said Merlin, but he said it lightly. 'I was having a bad dream…I think it was a dream.'

'What do you mean?'

'Oh, nothing. Give me a minute; I'm not properly awake yet.'

Austine, having got the fire going again with logs from a basket in the hearth, went over to the window to draw the curtains. She peered out curiously, and gave an exclamation.

'It's gone again, Julie – just like ours.'

'I beg your pardon?' said Merlin.

'The house,' said Austine, turning round. 'It isn't there – just water.'

'Oh – that,' said Merlin. He sounded relieved. 'It's called over-sailing. The top storey overhangs the moat. You'll see in the daylight.'

'So it really is a moated grange,' said Julie-Anne.

Austine pulled the curtains across and came and sat beside her. 'Hello, brother,' she said.

'Hello, sister,' said Merlin, and drew a whistling breath which brought on another coughing fit.

'As I was saying,' said Julie-Anne. 'Have you seen a doctor?'

'No. Should I?'

'The longer you're ill, the longer we have to stay here,' said Austine. 'If you ask me, it isn't us that need a guardian, it's you. Doesn't your father worry about you?'

'Have you met him?'

'Just fleetingly, in the hall?'

'Well then.'

'Mrs Bartle, what about her?'

'She looks after my father. You have to take your chance when you come here, you know. I'm sorry I had to bring you.'

'It's a good thing you did,' said Julie-Anne. 'Never mind, we'll look after you.'

'That'll be nice,' said Merlin. He looked at them thoughtfully under his eyelashes. The tension, which had receded a little, was suddenly back in the room.

'Did Sylvester tell you *how* I fell into the drain?' asked Merlin.

Julie-Anne looked at him gravely. 'He said you weren't quite sober,' she said.

'Is that all?'

'Why, was there more?'

'He didn't believe me...' said Merlin, half to himself.

'Didn't believe what?' asked Austine.

'Oh – nothing.' He sat up with a jerk, and swung his legs off the bed so that he was sitting beside them. 'I'm sorry I wasn't around when you arrived – I must have dropped off – I'm not feeling too brilliant, as a matter of fact. Did they look after you?'

'Your cousin, Sylvester did,' said Julie-Anne.

'Oh dear.'

'And I suppose the – is she the housekeeper, Mrs Bartle? She paid lip-service to hospitality, at least. But we didn't precisely feel that we were welcomed with open arms.'

'No, well, they live in their own world here. It revolves round my father, and anyone else, as I said before, takes their chance.'

'You certainly are,' said Austine, peering at him across Julie-Anne. 'You look awful – you should be in bed, wheezing like an old man of a hundred. We thought you were Frankenstein's monster.'

'Gee, thanks,' said Merlin. 'That's made me feel a whole lot better. Come to that, how about you?'

'Me?' asked Austine, startled.

'You've been crying. What's up?'

Austine had not been expecting such keen observation, neither had she been expecting the note of genuine sympathy and interest in his voice. After the chilly reception that the British Isles had given them, it took her off balance, and a lump rose in her throat choking her reply.

Julie-Anne answered for her. 'We were both feeling a bit far from home,' she explained. 'It was a plain attack of home-sickness. It is…a bit different here.'

A sudden flurry of wind and sleet against the window echoed the sentiment.

'Oh well,' said Merlin. 'I'll be all right again in a day or two, and we'll go home. I just couldn't drive the distance at the moment…I'm sorry.'

'Austine's right, you know,' said Julie-Anne, looking at him. 'You look like death warmed up. Why don't you just take to your bed and make the Bartles run round after you?'

'Because they probably wouldn't – and anyway, I shall survive, I've only caught cold.'

'We'll run around after you, then,' offered Julie-Anne. She slid off the bed and walked over to the fireplace, and stood looking down into the glowing logs. She had something on her mind. 'Did you…I mean, it must be an awful nuisance, having us dumped on you. Did you mind?'

'It came as a bit of a shock,' said Merlin, carefully. 'But I did ask for it, didn't I? And now I've seen you both, I feel better about it. In fact, I think I'm going to enjoy it.'

'You won't have Julie-Anne on your hands long,' pointed out Austine, who had herself in hand again. 'Just me.'

31

'That's right, just you. What do you want me to do with you?'

'Save her from Mr Achenbaum,' said Julie-Anne irrepressibly.

'The name sounds familiar. Who's he?'

'Daddy's agent that was, and one of the executors of the will. He wants her to be an actress on the films.'

'That sounds logical, on the face of it. Don't you want to be?'

'Not really,' said Austine. 'I'd like to be something more...more useful. A nurse, or something like that...'

'I see. Well, you aren't practising on me!' said Merlin, with decision. 'However, I see no reason why you shouldn't practice on other people, if that's what you want. We can look into it, if you like.'

Austine looked at him disbelievingly. 'You mean, you don't think I ought to follow in Daddy's footsteps? Everyone else always says...and my mother, too...'

'Hmm. My mother is your mother, and my father is a scientist, but that doesn't mean that I have to either dramatic or scientific. In fact, I'm not.'

Austine gave a sigh of relief. 'Gosh, what a relief! I've been afraid all along that Mr Achenbaum would get at you.'

'He hasn't tried yet,' said Merlin. 'If he does, I can easily find a polite answer for him – I assume I'm to be polite?'

'Oh yes – he's a dear really.'

A distant booming sound came from the depths of the house.

'The gong!' said Julie-Anne. 'Thank goodness – I'm starving. Let's not keep Sir Richard waiting, he doesn't like it.'

Austine jumped to her foot, and Merlin followed her, a little uncertainly. On his feet, he was as tall as his cousin, but where Sylvester was slim and somehow elegant, Merlin was big and rangy. Julie-Anne looked at him anxiously.

'If you faint on the floor, you'll stay there,' she told him. 'We'll never move you – are you all right?'

'Yes,' said Merlin, shortly, and shepherded them before him out of the room.

Dinner, much to the relief of Julie-Anne and Austine, who had wondered if it would match the house and their welcome, was plain but adequate, and excellently cooked, served by the silent Bartle. Although Merlin was quiet, saying little and eating less, Sir Richard bestirred himself to entertain his two unwelcome guests with the same old-world courtesy that had brought him from his studies to greet them. His conversation, as Julie-Anne remarked to Austine when they were back in their bedroom, was hardly exciting, but no doubt educational if you liked that sort of thing, and on the whole, she thought, he was rather a pet.

'He would be, if he didn't live on another planet,' agreed Austine. 'Just the same, I hope we don't have to stay here long – what an evening! The radio and *The Financial Times*, and no company but a silent guardian getting greyer and greyer by the minute, and only breaking the silence to cough.'

'That drain hasn't done him any good,' said Julie-Anne, and shivered. 'Do you think Mrs Bartle thinks of things like hot-water bottles? I'm frozen.'

Austine peered under the blankets. 'She does,' she said.

'Then let's go to bed and get warm. What with the draughts, and the cold, and the sort of damp feel of everywhere, I shall be wheezing soon!'

They climbed into the enormous, curtained bed and snuggled close together for more warmth. They lay for a little while, thawing and enjoying for the first time in their lives the indefinable charm of a bedroom warmed by an open fire, watching the firelight flickering redly on the walls and the polished furniture and listening to the soft sounds of the logs settling on the hearth and then, because they were very tired after the long day's travelling, they feel asleep. In the darkened room, the firelight died away to a soft glow, and outside the drawn curtains and the latticed window the sleet and rain gave way to snow, soft and slushy as yet, melting on contact with the wet ground, and blowing feather-light on the wings of the wind.

Julie-Anne woke in the early hours of the morning, because she was cold. Investigation proved why; Austine had rolled over and taken the bedclothes with her, leaving her sister more or less exposed to the elements, and the fire had died away to a few glowing embers. Shivering, Julie-Anne hauled the blankets back on to her side of the bed and tried to get warm. The hot-water bottle provided by Mrs Bartle had gone to a chilly, uncomforting rubbery cushion and was no help. She curled into a tight ball, wrapping her feet in the skirt of her nightie, and thought resentfully about centrally-heated bedrooms and warm, downy, continental quilts, and other luxuries conspicuous at present by their absence.

Sleep seemed to have gone for good. And now, in the dark, windy depths of the night, something else came back to Julie-Anne, something that she had pushed to the back of her mind and nearly forgotten. Merlin, with that lingering horror in his eyes, and in his voice, saying, '*I think it was a dream...*' And then again, later, withdrawing into his own thoughts and saying, so softly he had hardly been heard, '*He didn't believe me...*' That he was a lot more ill than he proposed to admit was obvious, but it did not quite explain either of those remarks. Nor yet did it explain the fact that when he had woken from that bad dream that might not be a dream, and heard Julie-Anne and Austine in the passage, he had not spoken or called out, or indeed moved from that tense, watchful attitude until they were right inside his room and he had actually seen them.

There was more in this tale about falling into a drain than met the eye, Julie-Anne decided, and whatever it was, she had a feeling that it wasn't very nice. One thing that Anabel had bequeathed to her son, whether or not he realised it, was her gift of creating an atmosphere with a look and a word, and that was just what he had done. He did not have to say that he was afraid of something, or someone, if 'afraid' was the word. He had woven the feeling into the air around him, and it wasn't until they had left the subject of the drain that the feeling had been dispelled.

Drain. It sounded faintly nasty, when one came to think of it.

It was no good. She wasn't getting any warmer, and not only that, she was going to have to go out into that freezing cold passage and visit the bathroom.

'Bother!' said Julie-Anne. She lay for a minute or two longer, trying to pretend that she was sleepy and warm and wasn't going to have to get up, but it was useless. She had to get out of bed, hunt round in the last of the fireglow for an inadequate dressing-gown and a pair of slippers of no practical value in this climate, and find her way to the bathroom, up and down the odd little stairs, round the corners, and without waking the whole household in the process.

She found the bathroom all right, even in the pitch-black night, although the experience made her resolve to buy a torch at the earliest possible opportunity. Raven's Dyke was inadequately supplied with electric light switches, and a young girl could come to harm falling downstairs in the dark. Worse than that, she found, on emerging from the bathroom, she could lose herself.

Julie-Anne stood in the dark and tried to remember which way she had come. She had turned in the right direction on leaving the bathroom, she was sure of that, so that the little flight of stairs and the passage that led to her bedroom must be on her right somewhere. Had she passed it?

Or not gone far enough? If she yelled, would Austine hear her, or would she bring the whole household out of their beds shouting for the fire brigade? One thing was quite certain, she couldn't spend the rest of the night standing where she was, because she would freeze to death. Feeling her way along the panelled wall, Julie-Anne crept on, fell smartly down three steps, and landed on her hands and knees. Ahead of her, she could now see a dim grey light. A window? But which window? The stairs? Or what? Julie-Anne got cautiously to her feet and crept on; there was only one way to find out.

Her slippered foot hit the end of the chest with a noise like the crack of doom, and her involuntary yelp of agony followed hard on its heels. Still, at least she knew where she was now, she had noticed the chest earlier against the banister rail at the head of the stairs. She sat down on it to get her bearings, hugging herself for warmth. Her teeth began to chatter.

The light went on so unexpectedly that she leaped off the chest.

'Good grief!' said Merlin. 'What on earth are you doing there?'

'Freezing to death,' said Julie-Anne crossly. 'I'm lost, and I'm cold, and I'm tired, and – '

'Sssh. That'll do, I get the picture. Where did you come from?'

'My bed,' said Julie-Anne. 'And if you don't know where it is, I'm sure I don't.'

Merlin began to laugh, and Julie-Anne looked at him distastefully.

'That's right, it's funny, isn't it?' What are you doing there, anyway, catching your death – if you haven't already, that is – laughing at people's misfortunes?'

'Sorry,' said Merlin. 'You can't sit there all night – come and thaw, and then I'll lend you a torch and you can find your way back to wherever you came from.'

'The proprieties...' murmured Julie-Anne, accepting the invitation.

'Just think of me as a father,' suggested Merlin.

Wrapped in an eiderdown in front of a fire with a good deal more life in it than the one she had left, Julie-Anne began to feel better.

'Did I wake you?' she asked, beginning to feel a little penitent.

'No. I was awake. Are you getting warmer?'

'Yes, thank you.'

'Good.'

A silence fell. Merlin, who had returned to a bed that looked as if he had

35

been fighting with it all night, stared into the fire with eyes that obviously did not see it, and Julie-Anne stared thoughtfully at him.

'Merlin,' she said, after a while.

'Mmm?'

'This evening, when we came in here first, you said something…you said Sylvester didn't believe you. Didn't believe what?'

He turned his head to look at her, but did not reply.

'You were talking about falling into the drain,' said Julie-Anne.

'Yes, I know what you mean.'

'What happened? How did you come to do such a stupid thing? Were you drunk?'

'No.'

'Then…look, tell me, for goodness sake! Don't just sit there looking like the family ghost! What happened?'

'Oh…I nearly was the family ghost. That's all.'

'What happened?' repeated Julie-Anne. 'Honestly, with this spooky house, and you, the only human being in it, spooked as well, it's enough to drive a person out of her mind!'

'Don't you think you ought to find your way back to your room?'

'No I do not,' said Julie-Anne. 'I want to know what it was you were dreaming about – 'She broke off. 'Don't look like that! Merlin, please! What on earth happened?'

Merlin did not answer immediately. He gave her a long, considering look, and found what he saw reassuring. Julie-Anne was no child, she was quite old enough to be her own mistress, and had none of the hallmarks of the too highly-strung that characterized his other ward. He came to a decision.

'It's a ridiculous story,' he said. 'Sylvester didn't believe a word of it, but if you want to hear it – well, here it is.'

'Good,' said Julie-Anne, and settled down to listen. She did not know quite what she had expected, but it was not what she got.

It had been one of those riotous Raven's Dyke evenings, so said Merlin, and unable to stand the pace any longer he had fled the coop and walked down to the village.

'I could have taken the car,' he said. 'But it was a fine night – beastly cold, with ice on all the puddles, but quite pleasant with it. It's only about three-quarters of a mile across the fields, but by car you have to go back up the road for a mile before you can turn off, and then it's another mile or so to the village. So I walked.' He paused, 'I went down to the pub – at least there's someone to talk to there, and the landlord, Tony Manners, is an acquaintance of sorts – I don't come here more often than I can help, so it's hardly a close friendship, but when I do come I tend to spend most evenings in the Lamb – you saw why tonight.'

'Yes,' said Julie-Anne.

Merlin had stayed in the Lamb and Flag until closing time, and when he had prepared to depart, Tony Manners had suggested he stayed on for an hour for a chat and a game of chess, and a quiet drink after hours. Since there was nothing to call him back to Raven's Dyke, he had stayed, and prompted by his friends' urgings, stayed and stayed, until he had finally torn himself away, refused an offer of a drive home, and retuned by the way he had come – along the bank of the River Whythe, on foot.

'The footpath goes along beside the river for about half a mile,' he explained to Julie-Anne, who, of course, had never seen the place. 'At that point, the drain enters the river via a sluice gate, and at the sluice the path turns off along the edge of the drain for a few hundred yards, crosses a footbridge and thence across the fields to here. I reached the sluice, all right, but…you know, Sylvester's right, it does sound ridiculous.'

'Go on,' prompted Julie-Anne. 'What happened? How did you fall in?'

Merlin looked almost embarrassed. 'Someone hit me over the head,' he said, evenly. 'After which, I presume they lugged me along the path and dumped me in the drain below the bridge, because the next thing I knew about anything, I was just going down for a third time.'

He paused to let that sink in, and Julie-Anne drew the eiderdown more closely round her.

'Go on,' she said, again.

'I would have drowned,' said Merlin, without emotion. 'I was in no state to help myself, but luckily for me, just at that precise moment, Tony came belting up the path and fished me out. We didn't talk about it then. Apart from having broken the ice as I went in, my head was going round and round, and between being completely frozen and half-concussed, I didn't really care about much else. I just went home – having said "thank you", naturally. But the next day…'

'The next day?' said Julie-Anne, when it seemed as if he was not going to continue.

'The next day,' said Merlin, 'I went down to the Lamb to have a word with Tony. He was so close behind me, he must have seen what happened, and naturally enough I wanted to know about it. But…and this is the silliest part…he said that when I left I was so thoroughly sloshed that he got worried, followed me, and was just in time to see me miss my footing on the bridge and plunge into the drain. He reached me in time to save me from drowning. And so on. I argued the point, of course, but he just gave me a funny look and offered me the hair of the dog. Well, I had a headache all right, but it wasn't a hangover. Nothing has a more sobering effect than chess. Hang it all, I know I was sober. I know I was attacked – murderously attacked – and…' He stopped, and a clouded, distant look crossed his face. The nightmare look. Julie-Anne stirred in her chair.

'Are you sure? Quite sure? I mean…well…'

Merlin looked at her. 'You too? Come here.'

'Why?'

'Come here. I'll show you why.'

Julie-Anne obediently got up and went over to him. He took her hand and put it round the back of his head.

'Feel that.'

'Pow!' said Julie-Anne. 'I'll bet that hurt.'

'It did. Now that, Miss Austin, is not a figment of my imaginations, drunken or otherwise. And if you can tell me how someone can hit the back of their head falling forwards off a footbridge, I'll be glad to hear it.'

'It wouldn't be easy,' admitted Julie-Anne. 'But it isn't impossible. After all, why should anyone want to hit you over the head and throw you into a drain? It doesn't make sense.'

'Oh, but it does,' said Merlin. 'At least, it does if I saw what I think I remember seeing…'

'What?' asked Julie-Anne. 'Don't – I don't know what you're seeing, when you look like that, but it gives me the creeps!'

'There was a boat,' said Merlin, in an odd voice. 'It was in the reeds, just below the sluice. I saw it from the bank. There was a man in it – lying in it. Someone must have just uncovered him and dived for cover when they heard me coming, because they wouldn't have left him in full view like that. Not…not the way he was.'

'How?' asked Julie-Anne. Merlin drew a breath which sounded rougher even than before. Julie-Anne, listening, could see the boat; see the man lying in it...

'Well, I won't go into details, but he had no face and no hands,' said Merlin, in a voice that sounded alarmingly matter-of-fact. He took another unsteady breath, which brought on another fit of coughing. Julie-Anne looked at him, and now the horror was in her eyes too.

'But that's horrible...'

'It was,' said Merlin, when he could speak again. 'Very. I keep dreaming about it, and – well, I just can't get it out of my mind. Well, would you?'

'Have you told anyone?'

'Not about the body, no. Only you. I told Tony and Sylvester about being attacked, and you know what they said. I thought of going to the police but...you see the problem.'

'Your friend Tony,' said Julie-Anne. 'His word against yours.'

'That's right. And me batting on a very sticky wicket. I'm not even sure myself...I know that sounds silly, but I only saw the – the thing for a split second. There's nothing there now – I looked – no sign of anything out of the ordinary. Nothing to prove I wasn't drunk, nothing to prove I was attacked but a bruise which I suppose I could have got in any one of a dozen ways, and Tony...well, it couldn't have been him who hit me, I'd have heard him coming, and anyway...he fished me out. I just can't seem to make sense of it.'

'If it made so deep an impression on you that you can't lose it even in your sleep, I'd say it was true,' said Julie-Anne.

'Thank you.'

'But – 'She broke off, and Merlin waited watchfully for her to continue.

'I don't know,' she said, at least. 'I think you should go to the police. You can't just...just overlook a...a faceless body in a boat.'

'Look,' said Merlin. 'My own cousin, who knows me reasonably well, is prepared to believe that I was so highly sloshed I didn't see straight – so far as the local police are concerned, I'm a stranger. Tony is local, well known, well thought of. Where does that leave me?'

'Your father – your family – '

'If it was Sylvester now – or Robin – or even my father, you might have a point. Me, in these parts, I'm the son of a wanton – but don't say so to Austine – a foreigner to boot. I cut no ice – except as I land in the drain.'

'Suspect?'

39

'No, I wouldn't put it as highly as that. Just not to be compared with the well-known landlord of the local.'

'Has anyone…well, gone missing?'

'No.'

'Oh goodness,' said Julie-Anne. 'I don't know what to think now…you are sure, aren't you? That you weren't – I mean that – '

'I know what you mean. Yes. Quite sure. What I'm not quite sure about is if I did see…what I thought I saw.'

'You ought to ask your friend,' said Julie-Anne, thoughtfully. 'He might have seen at least the boat…you don't know…'

'Julie-Anne,' said Merlin, gently, 'you can't have thought. If there was no boat, then you have to believe that I was drunk, because then nobody could possibly have a reason for drowning me. If there was a boat, then I was hit over the head. If I was hit over the head, then Tony saw it happen, but nobody hit *him* over the head. So, Tony is lying, or I was drunk. In the second place, you could say it serves me right. In the first place…do you begin to see?'

'Oh,' said Julie-Anne, suddenly grasping the point. 'It's his body – he knew it was there…he knew you were walking back and he kept you late, and – I see.'

'Late, but not late enough,' said Merlin. 'You've got it at last. And…well, I don't want to end up without a face. That's it in a nutshell.'

'Oh, Merlin! No – there's only one thing to do, isn't there?'

'And that is?'

'Get well, and get out. Quickly.'

Something of panic must have shown in her voice, because Merlin suddenly laughed and relaxed.

'That's a bit melodramatic, darling. So long as I seem to believe what I'm meant to believe, my face is probably safe enough.'

'That's all right then…'

'All right for me. What about the fellow in the boat? I dare say he was quite attached to his face too.' He gave an involuntary shudder, and Julie-Anne pulled the eiderdown close.

'So what are you going to do?'

'I don't know. I can't think. In fact,' he ended, in a sudden burst of honesty, 'just at present I feel so dammed awful, I don't care either. I just wish I could forget it, but I can't.'

Julie-Anne knew that she wouldn't forget it easily now, either. It was perfectly possible, of course, that the whole thing was the result of a fevered imagination, and it would be nice to believe it, for Merlin was undoubtedly a long way from well. But it was difficult to see why his imagination, in that case, should throw up such a picture.

A body in a boat.

A body with no face, and no hands.

A body…

IV

*'Between the acting of a dreadful thing
And the first motion, all the interim is
Like a phantasma or a hideous dream,'*
Shakespeare: Julius Caesar

The rest of the night passed restlessly for Julie-Anne. Although she found her way back to her room safely with the aid of Merlin's torch, and refilled the hot-water bottle in the bathroom so that she was warm enough, she could not settle. The macabre story that she had heard took possession of her mind so that she could think of nothing else. The uppermost thought that she had was that at all costs, she and Austine must be seen to hate Suffolk so much that Merlin would agree to their going south – even if she herself had to drive the whole way. She believed that he was right in saying that so long as he went along with the story that he was drunk and fell off the bridge he would be safe, for otherwise, her intelligence told her, Tony Manners would never have fished him out of the drain. What she did not believe was that he would be able to keep silent about it for very long. If he began to feel better, he would begin to think more clearly, and once he started enquiring too deeply into the matter his safety would be in jeopardy. Julie-Anne did not care particularly about the body in the boat, she had not seen it and she did not know who it was. It was a terrible thing, but a little like something read in the newspapers: it had happened to somebody else, could never happen to her. On the other hand, it could happen to Merlin, and she rather liked his face as it was.

It was beginning to get light before she finally fell into a troubled sleep, and almost at once, it seemed, Austine was shaking her shoulder and saying,

'Wake up, Julie, another exciting day at Raven's Dyke is just starting, and the fire has gone out and it's freezing!'

Julie-Anne rolled over and reluctantly opened her eyes.

'Whatever time is it?' She sat up. Austine was right, it was freezing. The fire, which neither of them had thought to bank up overnight, was cold grey ash, and the room was like a refrigerator. Outside the window, the sky was a yellowish grey and hung over the countryside like a chilling eiderdown.

'The weather forecast is awful,' said Austine, who was fully dressed and looking dreadfully wide awake. 'I've been down and listened to the radio. Snow in the north, and half the roads are blocked already, and it's coming this way.'

'Must you be so cheerful in the morning?' asked Julie-Anne, thinking fast. Snow blocking the roads didn't sound too good. She must get Merlin out of this place before it happened here.

'Snow!' she exclaimed, looking at Austine out of the corner of her eyes. 'I don't fancy being snowed in up here, we'll die of cold! Do you think we can persuade our guardian to drive south? He must have a car here somewhere, we can probably get there in a day, and I can share the driving.'

'I wish we could,' said Austine, readily. 'Let's try. If we've got to be snowed up with anyone, I'd sooner it was with Sylvester in London than Sir Richard and the Bartles.'

'We'll work on him at breakfast,' said Julie-Anne.

However, when they got downstairs there was no sign of anyone but Mrs Bartle. Sir Richard, she said, had had his breakfast and gone to his study to work. Mr Merlin was not down yet, and if the two young ladies would like to go into the dining room, she would bring them some nice hot porridge.

They ate their breakfast with one eye each on the window. A few half-hearted white flakes were already falling, and the wind had dropped. The ground was iron-hard, said Mrs Bartle, if it really came on to snow it would be treacherous after all the wet weather they had been having. She flitted in and out of the dining room with porridge and coffee and bacon and eggs, chattering cheerfully about various hard winters she remembered, and strengthening the girls' resolve to be gone as soon as possible.

Merlin did not put in an appearance at the breakfast table, and when they had finished, Austine suggested that they went and looked for him.

'For if we mean to go ahead of the snow, I think we'll have to do it this morning,' she said. 'Just look at it! The sky is full of it!'

Julie-Anne agreed, and they went upstairs and knocked on his door. A voice they hardly recognised invited them to come in, and they did so. One look at Merlin, and Julie-Anne realised, with an awful sinking feeling, that none of them was going anywhere. He was still in bed, and didn't look as if he could have got out if he had tried. The three of them looked at each other for a minute and then Merlin said, 'All right. Don't say it, I surrender.' He looked at Austine with what was almost a smile. 'You can practise on me.'

Julie-Anne went in search of Sir Richard to break the news to him and get the name of the doctor. She was more perturbed than she dare let Austine see; from the looks of it they were going to be at Raven's Dyke for some time – plenty of time for Merlin's conscience to get the better of him. It would have been nice to have been able to take Austine into her confidence, but she knew her sister well enough to realise that it would not be a good idea; Austine was highly impressionable, and to be snowed up in a moated grange with a potential murder victim would be nicely calculated to give her the heebie-jeebies. The whole affair was getting out of hand. Julie-Anne found herself longing for a sympathetic ear to confide in, but there was nobody in England she knew.

The doctor's name was Finn, and when Julie-Anne phoned him he promised to come round as soon as he could, but it was lunchtime before he appeared. He was young and cheerful and had an appreciative eye for pretty girls. Mrs Bartle took him upstairs, and Austine and Julie-Anne sat on the hall table and waited for him to come down again. Julie-Anne was by this time on the point of wondering whether she would tell Dr Finn what had happened – or what Merlin had thought had happened. A doctor should be reliable and sensible: he would be able to hand out sound advice. And a doctor so youthful was unlikely to have deep roots in the neighbourhood.

Dr Finn came downstairs again looking thoughtful, and joined the girls in the hall.

'How is he?' asked Austine.

'Lucky,' said Dr Finn. 'I should have seen him days ago. However, he's tough enough to throw it off quickly if you can make him be sensible. He's to stay where he is for a week, and we'll see; I've left a couple of prescriptions, presumably there's someone here who can go and collect them?'

He caught Julie-Anne's anxious look and smiled reassuringly. 'Don't worry, it's nothing dreadful. Nasty cold on the chest, not improved by neglect. He may be a bit delirious – delusions and nightmares and a bit of fever. It'll pass, don't let it worry you too much. I'll look in in a day or two and see how it's going.'

He was gone in a rush of cold air and a bang of the heavy door, before either Austine or Julie-Anne could do more than thank him.

'That's that, then' said Austine, sliding off the table. 'We're stuck. What would Mr Achenbaum say?'

'Wrap up warmly?' suggested Julie-Anne. 'Come on, let's go visit the sick.'

She followed Austine up the stairs feeling chilled with a cold that had nothing to do with the temperature outside. She was no doubt imagining things, but that reference to 'delusions and nightmares' had shaken her a bit. It could mean nothing, or it could mean one of two things: last night's encounter had been a nightmare delusion – or they had just been listening to a deliberate attempt to discredit anything Merlin might say about bodies in boats. Under normal circumstances, she would have taken the words at their face value. Under these circumstances, she suddenly realised with a shock, there was no one, from the doctor to Mrs Bartle, whom they could wholeheartedly afford to trust. Just herself and Austine. Because if the story was true… She almost told Austine then, but stopped herself in time. She couldn't tell her unless it became absolutely necessary.

They found Merlin in a contrite mood, lying back on his pillows and looking white and exhausted.

'I'm awfully sorry,' he said. 'You're going to be stuck here for weeks, from the sounds of it. I don't know what to say…' He broke off with a tearing cough.

'It isn't your fault,' said Julie-Anne. 'Is there anyone you'd like us to tell? What about your partner? He'll be wondering what's happened to you.'

'You could phone him for me, if you would – he lives down south in Aldmere – that's in Dorset, by the way –' He recited the number, and Austine wrote it down on the back of her hand with a pen she found on the dressing table. 'His name's Chase – Bob Chase. I'd email him, but there's no reliable signal in this wilderness in this weather. Poor Bob, he'll go mad…'

'Can't help his troubles,' said Julie-Anne. 'Have you got a laptop with you, then?'

'Yes, somewhere…downstairs, probably.' He made a face. 'I think I must have lost my mobile in the drain, last night, I can't find it anywhere.'

'Not to worry, we've got two – one each. Actually, you could just borrow one of them, if you can stop wheezing for long enough. And presumably your dad has a land line.' She picked up the doctor's prescriptions from the mantelpiece. 'What about these? Will Bartle get them?'

'Can you drive?' asked Merlin, through a further burst of wheezy coughing. He pulled a face. 'Sorry.'

'Me? Yes. Your father wouldn't let me drive the hearse, would he?'

'I doubt it, but you can drive my car, with my good will. It's in the garage. The two of you could go out this afternoon and have a look round before the snow comes down.'

Julie-Anne had already presumed the car, but it was good to be proved right. It was pretty obvious really: after all he had been going to Heathrow to meet them. If they weren't going to be stuck at Raven's Dyke, things might not be so grim.

'That would be nice,' said Austine, before her sister could reply. 'Do you really trust Julie? She's a demon on the freeway.'

'She'll have a job being a demon on the lanes round here,' said Merlin. 'The key's in the pocket of my coat, behind the door there. Mrs Bartle'll tell you how to get to Southwold, and there's a map in the car if you want to go farther.'

They took the key, made sure their guardian didn't want anything, and left him in peace: he looked as if he had had quite enough.

'Well, that makes it a bit better, anyway,' said Julie-Anne, looking at the key with satisfaction. 'At least we can go and look at some different wet countryside.'

'Perhaps this place Southwold has got a cinema,' said Austine. 'There's not even a television in this place. I wonder how long we'll be stuck here?'

'*Too long to be safe,*' Julie-Anne cried out to herself. Delirium, or fact? There was no way to be sure, but one thing she knew for certain, she would not have a moment's peace until they were all three of them gone from Raven's Dyke.

Julie-Anne telephoned to Merlin's partner. He didn't sound mad, merely remarking in a calm voice with a pleasing country burr overlying it that he was very sorry to hear that Merlin was ill, and to tell him not to worry. Everything was under control. Julie-Anne put down the phone feeling somehow surprised. It had not been a voice that went well with Merlin, the scion of an ancient house. But then, Merlin was very individual, owing more to environment than breeding. The image of a tough Canadian backwoodsman did not quite go with the ancient name, either. Anabel had a great deal to answer for.

As soon as lunch was over, Austine and Julie-Anne went round to the garage to find the car, which turned out to be a large green estate-car with a towbar on the back and a sticker on the windscreen saying ALDMERE SAILING CLUB. Julie-Anne was reminded suddenly of the girl who had become tired of taking second place to a boat, and of the fact, almost forgotten since she had learned it so long ago, that their guardian was now a professional boatbuilder. So that was what the voice on the telephone this morning had been; a boatbuilder. It suited him. It did not really suit Merlin.

Armed with Mrs Bartle's instructions, they found their way to Southwold without difficulty, and took the prescriptions to a chemist. Whilst they waited for them to be made up, they walked around the little town, and began to feel better about the British Isles. Even on a bitter winter's day, Southwold is charming, and both Julie-Anne and Austine were wholly American in their delight in the quaint and historic. They had tea in a pleasant little café before they left, and felt almost civilized again. Away from the gloomy house, Julie-Anne began to feel that even the unknown Tony Manners and the cheerful young Dr Finn might be telling the truth, and under the circumstances, with very little blame attached to Merlin.

Julie-Anne herself much preferred people to be reasonably temperate, but she knew that the world was wider than she had been allowed to find out, and people had widely differing standards. A sheltered life need not necessarily be an advantage, and in any event if Merlin chose to get what he described as 'highly sloshed' and fall off a bridge into a drain, he was the one who was now paying for it.

Merlin had been right about the lanes; Julie-Anne found them disconcertingly narrow and twisty, and drove the big car along them with great care.

'It feels as if we've been in England for ever,' said Austine, as they drove along. 'We only arrived yesterday.'

'A lot seems to have happened since then,' agreed Julie-Anne.

'Do you like him?' asked Austine.

'Who?' asked Julie-Anne, negotiating a particularly awkward bend with caution.

'My brother Merlin.'

'Yes…yes, I do. He's going to make a mighty strange guardian though. Do you like him?'

'Yes, I think so. I don't really know – hello, that must be the way to the village.' Austine leaned across the back of the seat and pointed. 'Down there on the right -you've passed it. The signpost said Whytham St Giles, 2½.'

'We'll go have a look at it if it's fine tomorrow,' said Julie-Anne. 'Don't let's cram too much dissipation into one day, or we'll run out of things to do. We're going to be here for a longish while, from the looks of things right now.'

As she spoke, the snow began to fall again.

It fell steadily, but not hard, for the rest of the day. Julie-Anne and Austine went to bed early, an evening at Raven's Dyke without even the doubtful company of a rather poorly guardian was highly sleep-inducing. This time, they took the precaution of asking Mrs Bartle how to keep the fire in, and having bought themselves a torch in Southwold, they had no undue disturbance in the night.

They awoke to a white world and a hard frost, and a long, cold, dreary day. It was too snowy to find the footpath across the fields without guidance, and Julie-Anne refused to take the car out on the grounds that the roads were treacherous and it wasn't her car. They divided their time between reading and re-reading the magazines they had brought with them, walking round the garden, and playing cards with an old pack they found in the living toom cupboard. Raven's Dyke was well stocked with books, but they were all either old or dull or of a scientific nature.

'This Sir Richard doesn't have a very lively time,' said Julie-Anne to Austine. 'No wonder he's so quiet.'

Austine stood at the window, staring out gloomily at the snow. 'He seems happy enough,' she said. 'I wonder what he and my mother made of each other; it must have been a …an unusual marriage.'

'It doesn't bear thinking about,' agreed Julie-Anne, thinking about it.

Austine left the window with a final shudder at the view and came and sat by the fire with her sister. 'If my father is Merlin's step-father… was Merlin's step-father…is Sir Richard any relation of mine?'

'Accessory before the fact, I should think,' said Julie-Anne. She picked up the cards and began idly shuffling them together. 'Funny, isn't it? I wonder what Daddy's thinking at this minute if he can see us. Who would have thought, when Hubert first mentioned it, that we'd end up here, like this.'

Austine yawned. 'What's the time? – oh Lord, five hours yet, before we can go to bed! Do you think he'll be better tomorrow?'

'Merlin? I don't know. If only something would *happen*!'

The day dragged to its close, long and boring and uneventful, enlivened only by mealtimes and occasional visits to their prostrate guardian. Nothing happened in spite of Julie-Anne's prayer. The only difference today was that Sir Richard, apparently feeling guilty about the quality of the hospitality offered by his house, sat with them in the evening. The fact that he was immersed in a heavy-looking book made his presence of no practical benefit, and the girls had another early night.

The frost held overnight, and no more snow fell. Mrs Bartle, at breakfast, reported that the main roads were clear and the snowploughs out in the lanes, and the forecast was that the frost would continue for at least another forty-eight hours. Hard on this news, the telephone rang, and turned out to be Sylvester for Julie-Anne.

'Hello,' he said. 'How's things?'

The very sound of his voice made things seem brighter.

'Humdrum…' suggested Julie-Anne, and heard him laugh.

'I thought it might be. Bob told me Merlin was laid low for a bit. How is he?'

'A bit better this morning, I think. He won't be fit for travel for ages yet, though.'

'Oh well. You can study architecture to pass the time.'

'Architecture?'

'Yes, why not? The house is a gem of its kind.'

'Oh…is it?'

Sylvester laughed again. 'All right, so you don't appreciate architecture. Never mind, help is at hand. Will you tell Mrs Bartle I'm coming up for the weekend, and get her to put a large fire in the grate and plenty of hot-water bottles in the bed? I'll leave work early and drive up, so I'll be along latish, and I'll eat on the way. If I tell her myself, she'll try and stop me coming, but if you tell her it'll be too late.'

'Sylvester – '

'Tell her I promise not to fall in any drains and be on her hands for weeks. Look, I must go; I'll see you this evening – '

He rang off before Julie-Anne could get a word in, and she put down her end of the phone and went in search of Mrs Bartle. The last two days had rather put the matter of the drain out of her head, but now it returned to her. Sylvester was one person with whom it would be possible to discuss it. She had not failed to take note of the fact that the doctor's predictions had not been borne out by events; Merlin had been – still was – very low-spirited and wheezy, but by no means delirious, and any bad dreams he might have had, he had kept to himself. That could mean nothing – or everything. Sylvester, at least, must know his cousin well enough to say which alternative was the more likely.

Sylvester, of course, already had said. He subscribed to the accident theory...but then, Sylvester knew nothing about any bodies, because on the telephone Merlin had hardly been in a position to tell him. She wondered uneasily what he would say when he knew the whole story.

Mrs Bartle greeted the news of Sylvester's projected visit much as that prescient young man had expected.

'Oh dear, dear, as if poor Sir Richard hadn't trouble enough to bother him,' she said, shaking her head despairingly. 'What with Mr Merlin poorly, and one thing and another, you would have thought Mr Sylvester would have more thought.'

'I think he feels that he can at least entertain Austine and me if he comes,' said Julie-Anne, diplomatically. 'Look I know you're busy, can't Austine and I get his room ready and everything? If you give us the sheets and things we can do it between us.'

Mrs Bartle looked at her with approval for the first time since they had made each other's acquaintance.

'That's very kind of you, dear, but it won't be necessary, I can manage, and Bartle'll do the fire. This house is so inconvenient...' She vanished into the back regions, still muttering to herself, and Julie-Anne betook herself upstairs, where she found Austine in her brother's room, trying to cheer him up.

'Hello, who was that on the phone?' asked Austine as Julie-Anne came in. 'I had an awful feeling it might be Mr Achenbaum checking up on us.'

'Alas no, no such luck. At least he might have rescued us. That was Sylvester.'

'Sylvester?' Austine's eyes lit up. 'What did he want?'

'He wanted me to break it to Mrs Bartle that he was coming for the weekend,' said Julie-Anne.

'And did you?' asked Merlin, with a lift of an eyebrow.

'Yes. She wasn't pleased, but as he said, it was too late by then.'

'Sylvester's no fool,' remarked Merlin, almost to himself. 'At least it'll make things a bit brighter for you two. I'm afraid I'm not being much good to you at present.'

'You're looking better, though,' said Julie-Anne, eyeing him consideringly. He met her look with a faint smile.

'I don't kill easily,' he observed, and Julie-Anne felt herself colouring. Austine looked from one to the other, questioningly.

'What's going on?' she asked.

'Nothing,' said Julie-Anne and Merlin, both together. Austine shrugged her shoulders and spread her hands.

'This place gets to you, after a while,' she said, severely. 'You want to watch it, Julie, you'll be down the drain next.'

'Heaven forbid,' said Merlin, and Julie-Anne gave a shiver.

Austine got up from where she had been sitting on the rug by the fire.

'Do you think if I went and twisted Mrs Bartle's arm, she'd let me make us a cup of coffee or three?' she asked. 'I haven't liked to ask her before, but I though this morning she was beginning to get used to us.'

'Try and see,' said Julie-Anne. 'She's definitely thawing, you're right. You might just be lucky, and I could do with one right now. I think this is the only really warm room in the house except Sir Richard's at this time of day.'

'I knew it wasn't just the pleasure of my company,' said Merlin in the voice of one making a discovery. Austine laughed and left the room on her self-imposed errand, and Julie-Anne sat down on the rug in her sister's place.

'Merlin,' she said, after a while.

'Yes?'

'When Dr Finn came the other day…you didn't say anything about what you told me, did you?'

'No. Any particular reason for asking?'

'Nothing about those beastly dreams you had, or anything?'

'No. What's it about? What's on your mind?'

'I just wondered...' said Julie-Anne.

'He's by way of being a pal of Tony's,' said Merlin, not realizing that by saying so he was being the reverse of comforting. 'He knew what Tony said happened, he didn't have to ask – so I didn't tell him. Is that all?'

'Yes,' said Julie-Anne.

Merlin looked at her narrowly. 'Are you sure? You looked kind of odd. He didn't say anything, did he? – no, of course he didn't,' he answered himself. 'Why should he? You're getting me so that I'm imagining things, young Julie-Anne, don't worry about it so.'

'Someone tried to kill you,' Julie-Anne reminded him.

'And changed their minds half-way. Remember that too.'

'If...' began Julie-Anne, but did not continue.

'You're still wondering if I was really drunk, aren't you?' said Merlin.

'Well...well yes, of course I am,' said Julie-Anne, in a sudden burst of honesty. 'I'm bound to, aren't I? You could have been, and dreamed the rest. I just wish I could really believe it, that's all. I just wish I could!'

Merlin looked at her queerly. 'What did he say – Dr Finn?'

'Oh – nothing,' said Julie-Anne.

V

'There is no private house (said he) in which people can enjoy themselves so well, as at a capital tavern.'
Boswell's Life of Johnson, 1776

The prospect of having Sylvester's company for the weekend put fresh heart into Julie-Anne and Austine, who had been getting understandably depressed. With this to look forward to, and the fact that Merlin was at least feeling well enough to like company by this time, Friday was not so bad as Thursday had been. They divided their time between entertaining their guardian and having snowball fights in the shrubbery, and finally came to the dinner table hungry, and in high spirits. Sir Richard found them excellent company that night, and was sorry when they left him to rejoin Merlin upstairs.

'This old house needs a little life in it,' he remarked to Bartle, before retiring back to his study, a remark so unprecedented that Bartle had recourse to the brandy decanter.

'For,' he told Mrs Bartle when he had returned to the kitchen, 'never did I think to see the day when Sir Richard would say such a thing.'

'Ah,' said Mrs Bartle. 'Even Sir Richard isn't proof against such pretty young ladies. American they may be, but they're no trouble, I must say. I shall be sorry to see them go.'

Julie-Anne and Austine stayed with Merlin until he fell asleep whilst they were having a sisterly argument about Mr Achenbaum – a character he privately longed to meet – then they tenderly tucked him in, turned out the light, and went downstairs to wait for Sylvester. Mrs Bartle was in the hall, looking undecided.

'Oh, Miss Austin,' she said, when she saw them. 'Mr Sylvester didn't give any idea of when he would arrive, did he?'

'Latish, he said,' said Julie-Anne. 'We'll wait up for him, if you want to go to bed, we don't mind. We're staying up until he comes anyway.'

'Well, it would be very kind of you,' said Mrs Bartle. 'Bartle and me is used to going to bed early, and Mr Sylvester, he has a way of getting held up. There's sandwiches on the kitchen table, I'll make a flask of coffee and bring a tray to the living room, he's always ready for a snack, that one.'

She brought up the tray ten minutes later, and said good night. It was ten o'clock. Two hours and a bucket of coal later a throaty roar made itself heard coming up the drive and faded in the direction of the garage. Peering out into the snow, the girls saw the shape of a very small car vanish round the corner of the house, and five minutes later Sylvester returned on foot with a suitcase and came indoors.

'Hi!' he said, dropping his suitcase, and gathering them both into a cousinly embrace. 'Beautiful as ever, I see! Gosh, what a journey, the roads are like ice! How's the invalid? Is Mrs B still up? I'm starving!'

'Hello,' said Julie-Anne, extricating herself from his arm gracefully. 'Of course. Are they? Asleep. No, but there's coffee and sandwiches in the living room, and eat them quickly, because we're tired and we're going to bed.'

There was a pause whilst Sylvester carefully unravelled this speech, and then he laughed gaily, and still with his arm around Austine, made for the living room.

Mrs Bartle had made enough sandwiches and coffee for all three of them, and they sat around the dying fire and exchanged news whilst they dealt with them.

'Poor old Merlin,' said Sylvester. 'Is he still insisting that he wasn't drunk? You wait until I see him in the morning he'd better have a better story than the one he told me.'

'Don't be mean to him, he's not at all well,' said Austine.

Julie-Anne said nothing, and Sylvester cocked an eyebrow at her.

'You don't believe that silly story, do you?' he asked. 'Good heavens, after an evening in the pub with Tony Manners, it's a miracle he didn't end up at the bottom of the Whythe! If you ask me, it's not fluid in the lungs, it's straight concussion that ails him – I mean to say, banged on the head in the dark? Whatever next – whoever would do such a thing? The invisible man?'

'Put like that, it does sound silly,' agreed Julie-Anne.

'Say, what is this?' asked Austine. 'I thought he fell off the bridge in the dark – drunk or sober, so what? It was just as cold.'

'You mean he hasn't told you?' asked Sylvester. 'Oh well, perhaps he's changed his mind. I'll ask him tomorrow.'

'But did he think he'd been hit on the head?' persisted Austine. Julie-Anne caught Sylvester's eye as he was about to speak, and shook her head slightly. He paused with his mouth open and then reached for his coffee.

'No telling what he thought, after five minutes in the drain,' he said. 'It's lucky Tony was there to do his rescue bit, that's all, or you might have been short of a guardian. I say, I wonder if he's willed you both to me?'

The moment passed in nonsense, but as they left the room to go upstairs to bed, Sylvester caught Julie-Anne's arm and held her back, allowing Austine to go ahead.

'You didn't believe it, did you?' he asked in a low voice.

'I don't know,' whispered back Julie-Anne. 'He didn't tell you everything. You ask him in the morning, but don't say anything in front of Tina, she doesn't know.'

'Why not? Julie, what else was there?' He fell naturally into the shortened version of her name that Austine used, which Merlin had never done so far.

'Ask him,' was all that Julie-Anne would say, and Sylvester, dissatisfied, had to leave for his own room uninformed.

At breakfast the next morning, he was so unnaturally quiet that Julie-Anne concluded he had already seen Merlin. It did not appear, either, that he had laughed the whole thing off, as she hoped he would. At the first opportunity, she decided, she would tell him what Dr Finn had said and see what he made of that, but the chance did not come that morning.

After breakfast they went up to see Merlin.

'Hello,' said Sylvester, with heartless cheerfulness. 'We've come to help you cough. I must say, I didn't expect to find you brought quite so low, but it must almost be worth it with these two gorgeous creatures to cherish you.'

'Almost,' agreed Merlin. 'Not so good for them, though. They've been playing patience to pass the time.'

'Well, I'm here to pass their time now,' said Sylvester. 'I nearly brought Winkie with me, but at the last minute I didn't think that Uncle Richard would forgive me, so I didn't.'

'Thank goodness for that!' said Merlin.'

'Why? She was very upset when she heard you were ill – perhaps she thinks you tried to commit suicide for her.'

'Don't be a fool!' said Merlin, crossly. 'She's got more sense, I would have thought.'

'All right, where's your sense of humour? No, seriously, she was upset – she sent her love and said she hoped you'd be better soon.'

'Thank her for me, then,' said Merlin, shortly.

'These lovers' tiffs,' said Sylvester, raising his eyes to the ceiling. 'Like living on a see-saw – oh well, no doubt my turn will come.'

'When it does,' said his cousin, viciously, 'I hope she treats you like a doormat, it'll do you good!'

'Ooh, nasty,' said Sylvester, with a grin. He looked at Julie-Anne. 'You wouldn't treat me like a doormat, would you, Julie? No, of course you wouldn't.'

Julie-Anne felt that he had scored off Merlin enough for one morning, and declined to play. 'What are we going to do this morning?' she asked. 'Tina and I'd like to go to the village: do you know the way across the fields?'

'Better than some,' said Sylvester, who did not seem able to leave his cousin alone this morning, and then, catching her eye, added hastily, 'I take that back, don't eat me. Yes, darling, like the back of my hand, but you don't want to walk, do you? I'll drive you.'

'You walk,' advised Merlin, moodily. 'It's safer.'

'We'll walk down before lunch, and have a drink at the Lamb,' said Sylvester. 'How's that?'

'Lovely,' said Julie-Anne.

'Unless,' added Sylvester, on a sudden thought, 'your guardian here is going to be sticky about Tina being under eighteen, that is. Are you?'

'I imagine you'll use what little discretion you have,' said Merlin. 'No, I'm not going to be sticky. For goodness' sake go, and the sooner the better.'

'We are in an evil mood this morning,' said Sylvester, to the room at large, and sat down on the edge of the bed with his back propped comfortably against the post. 'Sorry, Merlin. I take it all back. Jan and Bob said would you like me to take these two back with me, and they can stay in Douglas Road until you're better. Shall I? It'd be more fun for them than stuck here, and you wouldn't have to worry about them.'

Austine, who was in her usual place on the rug, looked up, alert and interested. Julie-Anne looked at Merlin. Merlin looked at his hands, and had a coughing fit to gain time. 'We can't leave him,' said Julie-Anne. 'Who'd cherish him then?'

'Mrs Bartle,' said Sylvester. 'And he's got a perfectly good father – well, a father, anyway.'

'Would you like to go?' asked Merlin. 'Bob is my partner, Jan is his wife. Bob and I build boats in their garage. They'd look after you till I got back.'

'Their house is like Clapham Junction,' said Sylvester. 'You certainly wouldn't need to play patience. And I could take you out in the evenings. What say you?'

'Would you like us to go?' asked Julie-Anne, of Merlin. He did not give a direct answer.

'You're not having much fun here.'

'You'd have even less if we went.'

'Austine?' said Sylvester.

'I'd love to go,' said Austine. 'But I think Julie-Anne's right. We ought to stay and look after Merlin.'

'Merlin? Look, he's your guardian, you're not his – oh well, have it your own way.' Sylvester laughed. 'No doubt you're right. Anyway, you've all weekend to decide, for I shan't go until Sunday evening.'

There the matter was allowed to rest for the moment. Julie-Anne felt a little bit mean, for she knew that Austine would dearly have loved to go back with Sylvester, quite apart from the increased social opportunities down in Dorset. But aside from the fact that it would be even meaner to leave Merlin to the mercy of Mrs Bartle, she had an irrational fear that if they left him, he could find himself in danger – and she had already decided that she would hate anything nasty to happen to him.

The three fit members of the party left the house shortly after eleven o' clock and set out across the snowy fields. Sylvester seemed to have thrived on his brush with his cousin, and kept his companions entertained with cheerful nothings as they crunched along. The famous footbridge over the equally famous drain was three fields away, but the land was so flat that they saw it long before they reached it, sticking up black and spindly against the white snow.

'Easy enough to fall off,' remarked Sylvester, as they paused on the edge of the frozen drain – a deep, narrow cut through the fields. 'Come to that, if it was icy you needn't even be drunk. I mean, look at it.'

Julie-Anne and Austine looked. It was a narrow, wooden structure raised above the level of the surrounding fields and reached by rickety wooden steps. A fragile handrail ran along one side, the other was unprotected. A skim of icy snow lay across the boards. Julie-Anne gave an involuntary shiver.

'What's up?' asked Sylvester, noticing.

'A goose walked over my grave,' said Julie-Anne. Sylvester smiled at her, and she had a feeling that he understood perfectly. Merlin nearly met his death here, and it wasn't a nice thought.

'Over you go,' said Sylvester. 'Mind you don't slip.'

The path turned left along the drain on the far side of the bridge, just as Merlin had described it, and led across two more fields to where the river, broad and grey and sluggish, flowed lazily between its snow-covered banks. At the little sluice-gate they paused again. The level of the drain, to the surprise of the two American girls, new to this type of country, was considerably higher than that of the river, and even above the level of the fields, running between steep banks. The river, too, was above the level of the fields, and it became more obvious to Julie-Anne how Merlin could well have been attacked without seeing who did it. Up until now, she had had reservations on that point in this flat and open countryside, but standing on the bank above the river things became clearer. Sylvester looked at her sideways.

'Well?' he said. Julie-Anne shivered again, and drew her coat closer. The boat must have lain just here, with its dreadful cargo, and the man must have hidden below the bank. If it was all true…

'Bleak, isn't it?' she said.

'Not too cheery at this time of year, I'll give you that,' said Sylvester, moving them along the path towards the village. 'These fen country rivers are much of a muchness, but it can be beautiful in the summer, if you like solitude.'

'I don't think I do much,' said Austine.

'I hadn't realized it was quite this low,' said Julie-Anne.

'Below sea level, a lot of it. The land is reclaimed marsh, and it's been gradually subsiding for the last hundred years.' Sylvester replied. 'The rivers don't subside with the land because they're running through flat lands and they don't go fast enough to scour out their beds – in fact, the coastline is constantly changing because of it, and the estuaries are never the same two years together. Some places even vanish completely. There was a town along the coast from here that was a flourishing little port, but its river silted up and the whole thing floated away. The trouble is, they drop everything, instead of carrying it out to sea. All the silt from the fields – debris from storms, anything. The Whythe, here, is a terror for it. If you want to dispose of anything – a body, for instance – you just chuck it in at slack water. The river just drops it in the mud, and that's the last you see of it.'

Julie-Anne looked at him in wide-eyed enquiry, and he gave a cheerful grin.

'If you had a body to dispose of, that is,' continued Sylvester, apparently enjoying himself.

'Is it tidal?' asked Austine, as they walked along.

'Oh yes – the sea is only a mile or two away. People keep boats at Whythe in the summer. It's a pretty little place with the sun on it, and leaves on the trees.'

'I'll take your word for it,' said Julie-Anne.

'If you get a heavy storm coming up behind the spring tides, it floods,' said Sylvester. 'That's one snag with the Whythe – among others. The tide comes up more determinedly than the river is flowing down, and then the river backs up all the drains and things, and the water spreads out all over everything. Gets a bit wet. If there's been a lot of rain, it's worse than ever, mucky, too. Shakes things loose. Nasty, damp country, and not at all the place for persons with a nasty cold on the chest.'

'There, I agree with you,' said Julie-Anne, in heartfelt agreement.

'I'm glad you do,' said Sylvester. 'Do you drive?'

'Yes.'

'Better and better. On reflection, you know, I think you're right to stay. But don't – er – how shall I put it? Stay too long?'

Austine had gone a little ahead. Julie-Anne pushed her cold hands into her pockets and tossed her hair back out of her eyes. She looked at Austine's back.

'He told you,' she said.

'Mmm. I'm still not sure that I believe it. Are you?'

'There's an awful lot of circumstantial corroboration.'

'That's very true, but don't get carried away. He did give his head a bit of a bang, and he is pretty sick.'

Julie-Anne was about to tell him what the doctor had said, when Austine, finding herself alone, stopped and turned round.

'Hi, come on!' she called. 'It's too cold to hang about!'

They hurried to join her, and walked briskly on until they came to the village.

Whytham St Giles was two lines of picturesque houses straggling down either side of a wide street that ended at the waterside. It stood a little higher than the fields, which, so said Sylvester, informative as ever, saved it from all but the worst floods.

'Even so, you don't keep the best Wilton downstairs in a hard winter,' he added.

The Lamb and Flag stood half-way down the village street, with a wide space in front of it on which stood one or two cars. It was a low, rambling place of much the same period as Raven's Dyke, and inside proved to have been sympathetically treated. The lounge bar, where Sylvester took his charges, was a pleasant place with dark oak settles, genuine dark oak beams, and a roaring fire. The landlord himself was behind the bar, and greeted Sylvester as an old friend. He was a pleasant-faced man of about Merlin's age, or a little more, with reddish hair and a ruddy, open-air complexion.

'We don't see much of you round here these days,' said Tony Manners. 'Nice to see you now.' He nodded to the two girls. 'Hello there.'

'Hi,' said Julie-Anne, trying not to look at him with too much interest. Austine, who had no hang-ups on the subject, greeted him openly, admired the bar, and came to join her sister by the fire. Sylvester joined them with drinks a minute or two later.

'Sherry for you, Austine m'dear,' he said, sitting down beside her. 'And even that is against the law, but I hope Merlin will call it "using what little discretion I have". He did get annoyed, didn't he?'

'You annoyed him,' said Austine. 'Thank you, sherry is fine. Is Winkie that girl you told us about, the one who got mad about us?'

'That's the very one,' said Sylvester. 'She was sorry she got mad, and also got around to thinking it wasn't so good having him stuck up here with you two. Jan is a friend of hers.'

'Why Winkie?' asked Julie-Anne.

'You might well ask. It's a bit better than Finuala, I suppose – you needn't think that Austine and Merlin have a monopoly of peculiar names. Other people's mothers have some funny ideas, too.'

'Yours, for instance?' asked Julie-Anne.

'Mine?' What's wrong with my name? Fine old family name – which is more than you can say for Merlin. He sounds like a wraith of grey smoke on a midsummer night, and when you look at him, it's even funnier.'

The outside door opened, and a man came in on a gust of cold air.

'Morning, Tony. How's things? A pint, please, and a packet of crisps. I'm starving.' He sat himself up on a bar stool, laid his wallet on the bar-top and looked around him while he waited to be served. There was only the group by the fire in the bar this early, and his look flitted over them casually, and then came to rest more firmly.

'Why, hello,' he said. 'Haven't I seen you two somewhere before?'

'On the hall table at Raven's Dyke?' said Austine.

'That's it! I knew I'd seen you somewhere. How is my patient going on? I meant to call in yesterday, but somebody went and had a baby on me.'

'He sounds terrible, but he looks better,' said Austine.'

'That's fine. Thanks, Tony.' Dr Finn paid for his pint and slid off his bar stool. 'Mind if I join you?' He sat down next to Julie-Anne, and nodded to Sylvester. 'Morning.'

'Good morning,' said Sylvester, a little coldly. 'Who's your pal, Julie?'

'Oh, I'm sorry, I thought you knew each other,' said Julie-Anne. 'Dr Finn – Sylvester Ravenscourt.'

'How do you do,' said Sylvester, formally.

'Pleased to meet you,' said Dr Finn. Tony Manners came and leaned on the end of the bar behind them.

'Merlin's all right, is he?' he asked. 'I hope I never see anyone as near drowning as that again.'

'He fell off the bridge, didn't he?' said Sylvester, casually. 'He seems a bit confused about it.'

'That's not surprising, either,' said Tony. 'Stoned out of his tiny mind he was, when he left me. Do you know, he came in here the day after under the impression that someone had slugged him. I ask you!'

'That must have been some evening,' said Sylvester, with a grin.

'It was,' said Tony. 'I'm sorry it ended the way it did, though.'

'It's lucky you followed him,' ventured Julie-Anne.

'Well, I did wonder,' said Tony. 'Getting better, is he?'

'Yes, I think so.'

'You want to get him back home as soon as you can,' said Dr Finn.

'This damp marshland won't do him any good, and it'll take him a while to get over this little lot. He'll be better out of that house, standing in the water like it does.'

'Funnily enough, we were just saying the same thing as we came along,' said Sylvester.

'Yes, well, you get him down south again. Far heathier.'

Was it imagination, or did he and Tony Manners exchange a significant glance as he spoke? Julie-Anne, who was facing the bar, could have sworn that something passed between them but like so many things in this affair, she was not sure.

The door opened again, and two men came in. Tony left his position at the end of the bar and went to serve them. Snatches of conversation reached the four sitting by the fire.

'We don't see many strangers around here,' Tony was saying. 'Staying around here, are you?'

'We hoped to stay here,' said one of the men, hitching himself into a more comfortable position on his stool. 'We're employed by the Catchment Board – checking the sluices and drains along the Whythe. Thought this would make a good base.'

'Well, I've a couple of letting bedrooms upstairs,' said Tony but not, it appeared, with any great enthusiasm. A sort of watchful stillness seemed to have entered the room. Dr Finn was apparently studying a set of hunting prints over the fireplace, but Julie-Anne had a feeling that he was deliberately listening. She became conscious of a faint pricking sensation at the back of her neck.

'That sounds splendid,' said the second man. 'We'll take them, if we may. We'll be out a lot of the time, so just bed and breakfast will do.'

'Fine, fine,' said Tony. He finished serving the two men, served another party who had come noisily in, and returned to the end of the bar.

'Place is getting properly overcrowded,' he commented. 'January, too. Those two chaps are from the Catchment Board.' He spoke to the company at large.

'Really?' said Dr Finn. He got up, and wandered over to the window, where he stood looking out for a moment or two before joining Tony at the bar. They exchanged another look.

'Well,' said Sylvester, looking at his watch. 'Time for another quick one, and then we had better be getting back. We don't want to upset Uncle

Richard, or Mrs Bartle might refuse to feed us. What'll it be, Julie? Doctor, you'll have one with us? How about you, Tony?'

The drinks were bought, and the conversation turned on non-controversial subjects. The bar was beginning to fill up now as it got nearer to lunchtime, and Tony soon had to leave them to attend to his business. A girl appeared from the back regions to help him.

'Are you going to stay on for a bit, or are you leaving with your friend here?' Dr Finn asked Julie-Anne. Sylvester was occupied with Austine. Julie-Anne answered evasively. 'We haven't quite decided. It depends on how Merlin is – he's our guardian, or my sister's at least. We'll go as soon as we can.'

'Ah. Good – that is, as I said, Ravenscourt would be better out of this marshy country. I'll be in to see him on Monday; will you still be there?'

Julie-Anne wondered if it was a deliberate trick question, or whether he was one of those people who never listened properly to anyone else.

'I told you, we haven't decided yet. We may be.'

'Well, if you are, I shall see you, I expect. Will you excuse me now? It's time I went home for my lunch.'

'Time, we did, too,' said Sylvester, catching this last remark. 'Swallow that sherry, Tina. Ready, Julie?'

They called goodbye to Tony as they left, and he raised a hand in acknowledgement.

'Bye. Mind yourselves on the bridge,' he called, with a grin, and they went out in the cold. A truck was parked outside the pub.

'Those two blokes, I suppose,' said Sylvester. He looked at Julie-Anne. 'What do you think?'

'What do I think about what?'

'Drunk or sober?'

'Look,' said Austine, falling into step beside them. 'You two have been talking in riddles all morning. Would you like to explain?'

'Riddles?' echoed Julie-Anne, and Sylvester said airily: 'It's nothing really, don't worry about it. Just a slight disagreement as to how my unfortunate cousin came to fall off the bridge – did he fall, or was he pushed, kind of thing.'

'Well, was he? Pushed I mean?'

'Of course not,' said Julie-Anne, crossly. 'Really, Sylvester, you are the limit!'

'Oh, very clever,' said Sylvester, softly in her ear, as they reached the beginning of the path. 'But what do you really think, my darling?'

'I still don't know,' admitted Julie-Anne.

'Didn't you get the feeling there was a lot too much insistence back there on his having fallen? I did.'

'No, no I didn't.'

'And what about your doctor friend with the roving eye? He seemed ready to urge you to take Merlin south in an ambulance, if need be. These dangerous marsh miasmas, you know…'

'Sylvester…'

'And what about the two Catchment Board blokes? Tony wasn't too happy about them, I thought.'

'What if he wasn't? Perhaps he's laid off his staff for the winter.'

'Oh, very neat! Oh well, have it your own way – but do be careful, won't you? I quite like my cousin and you and Austine are far too pretty to…lose face.'

'Stop it will you!' said Julie-Anne. 'I don't know what to believe – I don't know what you believe, either – but there's no need to give me the horrors.'

'All right, keep your hair on, my lovely. I'm only teasing…I think.'

'That's the bother of it,' said Julie-Anne, in a troubled voice.

'I know,' agreed Sylvester, suddenly sober. 'No, truthfully, Julie-Anne, I think it's all in the mind, or I wouldn't go back tomorrow; you do believe that, don't you?'

'Yes. Yes, I think I do.'

'Come along,' Sylvester took her arm. 'We'd better catch Austine – she'll be at us at again if we don't. I take it, we protect the child?'

'We do,' agreed Julie-Anne.

Hand in hand, they ran along the footpath in the wake of Austine.

VI

*'Tears, idle tears, I know not what they mean,
Tears from the depth of some divine despair.'*
Tennyson: The Princess.

Although she was still not quite certain whether he was serious or not, Julie-Anne was a little comforted by Sylvester's remark that he would not leave if he thought there was anything serious afoot. Moreover, she realized that she was losing sight of the fact that Merlin was plenty big enough to look after himself and his wards, if need should arise. She did not underestimate him: he might have fallen victim to a passing cold just at present, but he was no fool, and certainly no weakling. He did have though, she was forced to admit, a certain reckless air that make it a possibility that the popular version of the affair was true. He could have been, if not drunk, then sufficiently flown to be careless, and slipped on the bridge. That was the trouble; either story was so readily believable. She wished she know him better, and Sylvester too. She didn't find Sylvester foolish, and he could believe the drunken version; on balance, the sober version was the more incredible of the two. It was all very difficult. She tried to put it out of her mind.

Sylvester certainly did his duty by his cousin's wards. That evening he took them both out to dinner in Lowestoft, and on to the pictures, driving them in his middle-aged and noisy Mini. The evening was not a complete success in one way: two is company, three is a crowd, and although Sylvester was the perfect gentleman, his tact was not quite equal to the occasion; Julie-Anne began to feel a little superfluous. She sat in the back on the way home, snuggled into her coat and listening to the two in front laughing and talking together, to a background of music on the car radio, and became conscious of a gathering depression. She was glad to get home, and excused herself from coffee and sandwiches in the living room, left out for them by Mrs Bartle as before, on the grounds that she was tired, and betook herself to bed, but not to sleep.

The feeling was still with her the next morning, and when Sylvester suggested a drive round and another visit to the Lamb and Flag before lunch, she declined the treat, and instead went to sit by the living-room fire and be depressed all on her own.

Uppermost on her mind, for a change, she found her own affairs. What was going to happen to her, she wondered? A certain amount had been said about Austine's future, naturally enough since she was still so young, but nothing had been mentioned about her own. Where would she go, when she was free of Merlin's casual guardianship, and she had no further claims on him? What would she do? She had money enough, and time enough, to do anything she wished, but what did she wish? To return to the States? She thought of the old life, sheltered and secure, friends and outings and parties, her own car, a loving father. Austine...that was all gone, so much was certain. Six weeks, six short weeks, was all the time she had in which to decide. For the first time, it occurred to her to wonder whether her beloved stepfather had fallen a little short in his treatment of his daughters. Here she was, young, able-bodied, intelligent, wealthy, and totally unequipped to fend for herself. It was a sobering thought.

But then, she remembered, he had known he was going to die, he had kept them both close to him for that very reason...how hard it was to be fair, now that she had had time to stand back from the tragedy of his death and take stock. He had known he was going to die, and he had died, but here she was herself, now, all alone on the brink of – what?

A wave of black depression swept over, her, threatening to break in tears. This would never do. She would go and see Merlin, and talk to him, and perhaps she would feel better. Probably it was only because her sister was having all the fun. Stupid, really. She got up, and went upstairs.

She found Merlin immersed in the Sunday paper. He was a lot better today, and threatening to get up after lunch, but he still sounded dreadfully rough. He put the paper down when she came in and sat on the end of his bed.

'Hello – I thought you'd gone out.'

'I decided not to. I felt a bit like a chaperon, and it didn't really suit me.'

'No, you don't look the part.' He smiled at her. 'I must remember to tell that sister of mine to kick him around a bit. It'd do him some good if someone did.'

'Anyone would think that you two didn't like each other,' said Julie-Anne.

'We haven't a great deal in common. He's a bit of an idiot.'

Julie-Anne remembered something and laughed. 'He told us that you were mad as a March hare.'

'Gratifying, I'm sure.' He studied her carefully for a moment. 'What's up with you anyway? You look a bit down.'

'I am a bit. I was thinking…'

'About anything in particular?'

'Me. What I'm going to do with myself.'

'Reach any conclusions?'

'No.'

Merlin lay back and flung the paper on to the floor. 'All right, let's talk about it. Have you any hereditary talents, or are you like Austine and me?'

'None.'

'Austin Willerby wasn't your father, was he? I seem to remember him calling you his stepdaughter.'

'That's so. If I was his daughter, I'd be Julie-Anne Willerby.'

'True. Was your mother an actress too?'

'No. She wasn't anyone really.' Julie-Anne frowned in an effort to bring back the shadowy figure. 'I don't remember her much. My father was an airline pilot, he was killed before I was born; I think she had been a court stenographer, but I was never really sure. I remember being furious when she married Daddy, but it didn't last. He was such a larger-than-life person, and she was a little brown mouse…'

'Well, no one would expect you to be an airline pilot, and you're definitely not a little brown mouse…so that leaves you a pretty wide choice. Haven't you any ideas?'

'No. It's always been so easy for me, and for Austine. She's got more ambition than I have. I just don't know.'

'You could get married. Ever thought about it?'

'Often, of course I have. Every normal girl does, I suppose.'

'Nobody in view?'

'Nobody.'

'Good heavens!' said Merlin. 'What's the matter with the American male? You're what – nearly twenty-four? Nobody *at all*?'

'I've had boyfriends,' said Julie-Anne, half-defensively. 'Nobody serious… at least…' She stopped. An awful sensation of striking out into waters too deep for comfort came over her. 'How did we get on to this subject?' she asked, indignantly.

'By gradual degrees. What's the matter? Have you remembered some highly unsuitable suitor from whom I will be forced to withhold my consent?'

'No – '

'Then what? You look like somebody caught in the act of crime.' His eyes narrowed suddenly. 'You haven't fallen for that ass, Sylvester, have you?'

'I – '

'Because if so, what are you doing sitting there? Get out and fight, my girl. Austine doesn't need him, she's far too young.'

'No, no – not Sylvester. I mean…'

'Whoops!' said Merlin.

There was a long silence, while grey eyes looked into blue. The blue looked away first. Julie-Anne felt herself blushing furiously, and could have kicked herself. What a moment to make a discovery like that. What a ghastly, inauspicious moment. And how dared he, how *dared* he, see the very moment of discovery?

After a minute or two, she ventured to steal a look at him, and was indignant to find that he was not even looking at her, but staring at the window with a far-away look in his eyes. Well, she thought, with a certain satisfaction, he'll have a job to talk around that one without putting his foot in it. Let's just see him try, that's all!

A minute or two later still, it began to dawn on her that if anyone was going to say anything it would have to be herself. Merlin appeared to have gone into a trance.

'How about you?' she asked, carrying the war into the enemy's camp. He came back to earth looking startled.

'Me? What about me?'

'We were discussing my love life,' Julie-Anne reminded him. 'Yours seems to have taken a turn for the better, from what Sylvester said.'

'Oh. You mean Winkie MacKenzie.'

'Mmnm. Are you going to marry her and make her to be a mother to Tina?'

Merlin looked as if this was going rather too fast for him. He hedged, with what Julie-Anne could only admire as great skill.

'I don't think she's the motherly kind.'

'She sounds tender-hearted.'

'Winkie? Does she?' He sounded as if the idea was new to him.

'She didn't like you being ill.'

'Ah. That. Well, there's something rather romantic, I suppose, in the thought of a fellow laid on his death bed. The Barbara Allen touch.'

Julie-Anne was unacquainted with English folk songs; her education, admirable as it was, had omitted them. She said nothing.

'Come here,' said Merlin.

'Why?' asked Julie-Anne, but she came just the same, and put her hand in his outstretched one as trustfully, she thought resentfully, as a silly kitten.

'How long is it before the ties your – our, I suppose I should say – our step-father bound us with are broken?'

'Six weeks, give or take a day.'

'Six weeks. That's a reasonable time. Stick around, and let's see what happens, shall we?'

'Happens?'

'Yes. We can see how far the today-my-true-love-died-for-me-I'll-die-for-him-tomorrow bit takes Miss Finuala MacKenzie. It should be interesting.' He raised her hand to his lips and kissed it fleetingly. 'Then you can dance at my wedding.'

'That'd be fun,' said Julie-Anne, lightly, but inside her head she thought, chief mourner, more likely.

'Do you do crosswords?' asked Merlin, after a pause, and it was such a non sequitur that Julie-Anne looked startled in her turn.

'Crosswords?'

'Yes. There's one on the back page of that paper you're standing on.'

'Oh...sorry.' Julie-Anne picked it up hastily.

Sylvester and Austine came back and found them deep in the crossword, their two fair heads together over the dictionary, laughing as if nothing had passed between them.

VII

*'There was a roaring in the wind all night;
The rain came heavily and fell in floods.'*
   Wordsworth: Resolution and Independence

Sylvester left Raven's Dyke in the early afternoon, earlier than he had intended. The hard frost was showing signs of breaking, and heavy clouds promised further snowfalls. He kissed Austine in a cousinly fashion when he left, for Julie-Anne and Merlin were both present at their farewell, and if Austine's eyes were a little bright, nobody noticed too closely.

'See you all at the weekend, if not before,' he said. 'Don't forget to let us know when you're coming, or Robin and I will have worse trouble with Mrs Fanshawe than you ever had with Mrs B. Take good care of yourselves.'

He was gone in a roar of exhaust, and the three who were left repaired to the living room to finish the crossword.

It all seemed so simple at that moment. If the weather stayed clear, they planned to leave Raven's Dyke on Wednesday or Thursday, and with Julie-Anne and Merlin sharing the driving expected to be able to make short work of the journey to Dorset. Any possible bodies, much to Julie-Anne's relief, would be left behind in Suffolk, firmly stuck in the mud at the bottom of the Whythe. Finished. Unfortunately, it did not quite work out like that.

Monday dawned with a fresh, and heavy, fall of snow. The snow came down, and Merlin's temperature went up, soaring merrily away in the hundreds again. Both snow and temperature came down on Tuesday, and on Wednesday the snow ceased, but Merlin's temperature went up again.

'This is silly,' said Julie-Anne. 'What's the matter with you? We'll be here for ever at this rate!'

Dr Finn, rather gloomily, Julie-Anne thought, said it was nothing out of the way.

'But we can't travel?' said Austine.

'Not really, I couldn't advise it.'

'How long?' asked Julie-Anne, with some foreboding.

Dr Finn hesitated. 'We'll just have to wait and see,' he said. 'The lungs are clearing nicely – just wait and see.'

He had lost a lot of his friendliness, it seemed to Julie-Anne, and wore a preoccupied air. She told herself that perhaps he was overworked. Ever since it had dawned on her that she had at last met the one man in all the world that she would like to marry, she had been unduly sensitive on the subject of Merlin, jealous of every look and word, or even a cough or a wheeze. Winkie, whoever she might be, would never value him so well.

They waited and saw. Merlin, more browned off with things than any of them, got up when he felt like it and went back to bed when he didn't, and became more and more irritable, and in the meantime the weather began to change. The air turned suddenly softer, and the wind began to get up. By Thursday morning, there was a definite thaw on the way, and the wind was approaching a gale. On Friday, the snow was melting rapidly, it was raining hard, and there was an undeniable force-eight gale blowing.

'Any minute now, and you'll find out what the moat is for,' said Merlin. Mrs Bartle was more explicit.

'All this snow melting, and the spring tides due, and this gale,' she said, worriedly. 'We'll be having the floods out.'

Julie-Anne remembered what Sylvester had said about floods shaking things loose, and her heart sank. She was not helped by the fact that the more the rain fell, the more withdrawn Merlin became; he obviously had something on his mind – Merlin, of course, was as familiar with the peculiar properties of the Whythe as Sylvester. She had never doubted that he had believed that he had seen what he had thought he had seen, but for the first time she found that she herself was beginning to have a firm opinion of her own. It was not just bias, however much she tried to convince herself that it was. She no longer believed, or thought she could believe, that Merlin had been drunk that night. He had been, if not stone cold sober, sober enough to know what happened to him. She wondered how long things had to be in the bottom of the river before the mud had claimed them for ever.

71

On Friday afternoon, following a suggestion that came rather surprisingly from Sir Richard, Julie-Anne and Austine took Merlin's car and drove down to the sea. Due to the vagaries of the weather they had not visited the coast since their arrival in Suffolk, apart from the afternoon they had spent in Southwold. It was a frightening sight. They parked the car and got out to take a better look, for with the car windscreen covered with salt spray it was difficult to see. The wind nearly took them off their feet, and, laughing and holding on to each other for support, they staggered among the dunes and crouched down in the shelter of the largest one they could find. Sand and spray flew round them, and the marram grass on the tops of the dunes was blown flat, steaming silver in the gale. Ahead of them, the North Sea was boiling green-white to the horizon. Neither of them had seen a sight like it in their lives.

'It's magnificent!' exclaimed Austine, and the wind took the words and whirled them away, so that Julie-Anne, close as she was, shouted, 'What?'

Austine put her mouth close to her sister's ear. 'Magnificent!' she bawled.

Julie-Anne could just imagine the force of the sea, with a high tide behind it, sweeping up the Whythe and scouring the channel in a reverse direction, throwing up who knew what.

'I'm freezing,' she shouted. 'Let's go back!'

They staggered back, and collapsed in the blessed haven of the car, breathless and windblown.

Julie-Anne drove to Whytham St Giles. She wanted to see what the river looked like, and Austine was agreeable. It was blowing like smoke even inland. The river, dark and muddy and higher than they had ever seen it so far, swirled evilly against its banks; Julie-Anne and Austine stood at the end of the street and looked at it.

'Suppose it does flood,' said Austine. 'Do we take to the boats, or what?'

'Merlin says the moat takes all but the very worst floods,' said Julie-Anne. 'I suppose the roads may get covered – I've a feeling that we're going to find out anyway.'

They walked along the bank as far as the sluice; it was wide open and the water from the drain, creamy and turbulent, poured out into the Whythe. The sluice was only just taking it. Three or four serious-looking men were standing there looking at it, and as the girls approached, one of them broke away from the group and came to meet them. It was Tony Manners. He looked a very worried man.

'Hello there, what are you doing around here on a such a foul day?' he greeted them.

'Taking a look,' said Julie-Anne. 'Is it going to flood?'

'It looks pretty bad. The river's up to the level of the drains already, and the ground is still saturated. If I was you, I'd get down south while the going is still good. It's going to be bad up here come the weekend, when the spring tides come in. The river's backing up already as far as the village, and the tide's got ten feet to go yet.'

'That's bad?' asked Austine.

'That's bad. Even if the rain stops – and it doesn't look as if it's going to – there's bound to be a certain amount of flooding. There's an efficient heater in that thing of Merlin's, can't you get him out of here?'

He found he was talking to Austine only, for Julie-Anne had walked past him up to the sluice, and was in conversation with the men there. He muttered something and went after her.

The men were all from the village; the two men from the Catchment Board could well be looking at another sluice somewhere. It was silly to expect them to be at this particular one. Julie-Anne turned away and walked back towards Austine; she met Tony on the way.

'I should get home if I were you,' he shouted above the roar of the water from the drain. 'It's coming in nastier than ever. Get back to Raven's Dyke!'

'Just going,' yelled Julie-Anne. 'There isn't anything we can do to help, is there?'

'Just get back – get down south if you can. I just told your sister. Get away.' He called the last words over his shoulder as he strolled back up to the sluice. Julie-Anne rejoined Austine, who between the wind and the rain looked half-drowned but exhilarated, as if something within herself had risen to meet the excitement and the danger.

'This is fantastic!' she shouted to Julie-Anne, as they almost ran back to the car on the wings of the wind. 'I wouldn't have missed it for worlds! What's going to happen, did those men say?'

Julie-Anne flattened herself against the car to allow passage to a lorry loaded with sandbags, before opening the door and diving in out of the wind again. Austine got in beside her, it was a relief not to have to shout at each other.

'It's going to be dampish,' she replied, pushing her soaking hair out of her eyes and fitting the key into the dash. 'I think we go back to the house and stay there. I don't believe it's going to be all that much fun for a day or two.'

Along the lane they passed the Catchment Board truck, pulled into the road behind a police car. The two men, and a third who must have been in the car, stood talking under the lee of a hedge. All three looked up as the big car nosed past, and Julie-Anne, watching in the mirror, was uncomfortably conscious of eyes following them until they rounded the bend out of sight.

All night long, the wind roared around the old manor house, and the rain dashed in sheets against the windows. It was cold with a completely different kind of cold to that which the snow had brought, a cold that got into the very bones. Austine and Julie-Anne, huddled together in the great half-tester, lay awake listening to the rude battering of the elements and slept but fitfully. All the next day, the rain and the gale continued. Dr Finn came up in the morning, unheralded and unexpected, but no doctor in his senses would have suggested that Merlin drove several hundred miles through that storm. He left looking a lot paler than when he had arrived.

The tide swept in again, a little higher yet. Sunday morning, around four o'clock, would see the top of the springs.

Once more the night was wet and stormy. The high tide, with the gale behind it, came forcing its way up and the slow-flowing Whythe was forced back and back, up to the sandbag reinforcements, up and up through the ditches and the drains, until the water, having nowhere else to go, spilled over and spread across the fields. And still the relentless tide churned its way up the river, stirring the mud, loosening debris, spreading its sludgy harvest along the banks until at last the thick clinging mud at the bottom of the river was forced to loosen its hold on the dreadful thing that had lain there and it floated to the top to end up lodged among the reeds by the slowly falling tide, where men could find it.

Owing to the heavy flooding, which held up those usual news-carriers, the milkman, the baker and the postman, there was no warning at Raven's Dyke of what had happened. The first thing any of them knew was just as they were sitting down to breakfast, when a car came flying up the drive in a cloud of spray and pulled up outside, and a man came leaping out and hammered furiously on the door. The family in the dining room exchanged surprised looks over their cornflakes, and there was a pause in the conversation – desultory at its best at that hour of the morning – whilst everyone listened to Mrs Bartle trotting across the flagged floor of the hall and opening the door. Sounds of agitation and remonstrance could be heard, and Sir Richard tut tutted to himself. He was a man who liked peace and order and meals eaten at a leisurely pace in an atmosphere, at worst, of long quiet pauses in civilized conversation. Fond as he was of his son and his two American wards, he privately owned to a longing for the return of his uninterrupted solitude, and violent altercations in the hall at breakfast time were, he was inclined to feel, the last straw. Julie-Anne, who was beginning to be fond of him, gave him an understanding smile and rose to her feet.

'I think I had better go and give Mrs Bartle a little backing,' she suggested. 'I won't be a moment.' She had to make an effort not to leave with undignified haste, for she had recognized the voice in the hall. Suddenly all the half-disbelieved horror had become real and nightmare breathed coldly on her neck.

Tony Manners had pushed past Mrs Bartle and stood in the middle of the hall, giving every appearance of a man distraught past thinking.

'But I must,' he was saying. 'You don't realize how important – ' He broke off and swung round as the dining-room door opened, a sudden hope in his eyes which flickered and died when he saw it was only Julie-Anne.

'Hello, Mr Manners,' said Julie-Anne, pulling the door closed behind her. 'This is an early call, isn't it? We're just in the middle of breakfast.'

Tony Manners took a step towards her. 'Look, I must see Merlin – it's vitally important. This – ' he hesitated, and settled for ' – lady, says he isn't available, but surely he must be. I must see him.'

'I told him Mr Merlin was ill,' said Mrs Bartle, in the background. 'But take no for an answer he won't, not from me. Perhaps you can persuade him, Mis Austin.'

'That's all right, Mrs Bartle,' said Julie-Anne. 'I think Merlin would want to see him. I'll take him up, shall I?'

'It isn't a reasonable hour for making calls,' said Mrs Bartle, with a sniff redolent of disapproval. 'However, if you say so, Miss Austin, I'll show the gentleman up myself.'

'Don't you worry,' said Julie-Anne, 'Sir Richard will be wanting his coffee. You see to him, I'll look after Mr Manners.'

'Thank you, Miss,' said Mrs Bartle, and left, with a cold look at Tony.

'Come on,' said Julie-Anne, and led him up the stairs. She was not at

75

all sure what had happened – although she had a grisly suspicion – but a further act in the drama was quite obviously about to take place. She wondered uneasily where it would lead.

In the passage outside Merlin's room, she paused. 'You wait here,' she said to Tony. 'I'll just make sure he's awake – I won't be a moment.' She did not give him a chance to answer, but whisked herself speedily through the door and shut it firmly behind her. Merlin, who was wide awake as it happened, fully dressed for the first time since she had met him and sitting beside his fire with his laptop, looked at her in surprise as she ran across the room and knelt beside him.

'Sssh,' she whispered. 'Keep your voice down. There's Tony Manners outside the door in a state. What shall we do?'

No one had ever called Merlin stupid.

'Oh, Lord,' he said. 'I was afraid that might happen.'

'I wondered too, yesterday, when I saw the river,' said Julie-Anne. 'What do we do? He insists on speaking to you, and he'll come banging in here any minute.'

'Let him come,' said Merlin, thinking quickly. 'Can you manage not to shut the door as you go out? Stay in the passage and listen.'

'He'll notice – '

'We'll have to chance that. Look – draw the curtains across a bit on that side of the bed and make sure the latch makes a noise – quick.' He closed his laptop and set it aside, and as Julie-Anne jumped to her feet, and ran round to the door side of the bed, she spoke in her normal voice. 'All right, if you're sure, I'll get him. I won't be a moment.' She put out her hand to the door latch, but it was lifted as she moved and the door flung open. 'Look here,' said Tony Manners, striding through it. 'This is important – I can't wait about all day.'

'Good morning, Tony,' said Merlin, cheerfully; he must have moved like lightning, for he was lying on the bed looking frail, with the blankets pulled over his trousered legs. Julie-Anne left the room, drawing the door close behind her. She lifted the latch and allowed it to fall into place again with the door still slightly ajar. Leaning against the door post with her ear to the crack she heard Tony cross the floor, drawn by the attraction of a log fire on a bitterly cold morning. That meant he could no longer see the door at all now the curtain was drawn. She settled herself to listen.

At first there was a long silence, and she could imagine that Tony might well be stuck for words to begin; it must be a little awkward for him, after he told everyone that Merlin was drunk on that momentous night, to have to come back to him for…for what? Help? It hardly seemed likely, for surely he could safely stick to his original story. Drunk, Merlin could be supposed to have seen his body anywhere, presumably. He could be shown to be so confused about the events of the night that almost any explanation would be likely. Julie-Anne herself could think of several plausible ones. Tony only had to sit tight and keep repeating himself… and then, at last, he broke his silence.

'I saved your life,' he said, diffidently.

'Yes,' agreed Merlin, and waited for what might come next. Tony shifted awkwardly and leaned his arm across the mantelpiece, looking down at the blazing logs in the grate, anywhere but at Merlin.

'They wanted to kill you,' he said.

'With, or without a face?' enquired Merlin. Tony shuddered.

'It was natural causes, I swear it,' he said. 'You must believe that – if you believe that, you don't have to say anything about it, do you?'

'It didn't look very natural to me.'

'It was, I tell you. He just died – I suppose it was his heart or something. I don't know. But he wasn't murdered, I swear to God he wasn't. You don't have to say anything. Promise me you won't – please, Merlin, you've got to.'

'If he wasn't murdered, how did he get to where – and how – I saw him?'

'Oh, that – that needn't concern you surely? It's no business of yours if he wasn't murdered – it can't be. It mustn't be.' Tony's voice broke with urgency; Julie-Anne, on the other side of the door, thought he was near to tears. She began to be very frightened indeed.

'Of course it concerns me,' said Merlin, with unwonted warmth. 'Natural causes or not – I saw him, Tony! If he died of natural causes, what need was there to do…what was done?'

'It couldn't hurt him. He died, I tell you.'

'He certainly did,' said Merlin, grimly. There was a pause. When Tony spoke again, his voice was so low that Julie-Anne hardly heard it.

'Merlin – look, I can't explain…but I saved your life. Without me you would have been drowned. I know it, you know it. You owe me your life… well, mine is in your hands now. You can save me now. You don't have to do anything, it won't cost you anything. Just let my story stand, and go home. No one'll ask you, you won't even have to lie. Just be quiet, and get out. I beg you, Merlin, please!'

Merlin made no reply, and after a pause, Tony spoke again, very low but Julie-Anne caught the words.

'Merlin – please!' There was a world of pleading in his whisper.

'Look, Tony,' said Merlin, and for the first time there was hesitation in his voice. 'I fully realize that without you I shouldn't be here now, and for that, believe me, I'm grateful. But you must see – you must see – that if you saved my life a dozen times over, I can't just forget what I saw. The very fact that you're here makes it even more impossible. Who was he? Why was his body so mutilated? What is it you're trying to make me help you hide?'

This time there was no mistake about the tears, the man could hardly speak. 'Oh, God, I curse the day I met you...I wish I had left you to drown that night...'

Footsteps ran across the wooden boards, and Julie-Anne jumped back and flattened herself against the wall as the door was wrenched open. Tony Manners never noticed that it had not been shut, or Julie-Anne outside it. He pushed past her without seeing her, blind and beside himself, and she was never again to forget his face as she saw it then.

There was nothing to be gained by following him, he was already more than half-way down the stairs, and a minute later she heard the heavy slam of the front door. Slowly, she went back into Merlin's room.

Merlin was looking thoroughly shaken, as well he might. Julie-Anne sat down on the edge of the bed.

'The plot thickens,' she said.

'It does indeed,' agreed Merlin. 'Julie-Anne – why have I got this awful feeling that I've just started something that's not going to be easy to stop?'

'Because you have,' said Julie-Anne, hardily. 'He was afraid for his life.'

'I realize that.'

'Merlin...'

'What?'

'Couldn't you have promised him...what he wanted? He did save your life.'

'Mine, yes. What about the one who died of "natural causes" and was flung into the river once he had been rendered unidentifiable? That wasn't done for nothing, natural causes or no. How can I condone something that I don't even know what it is? Could you?'

'If he's in danger, so are you.'

'While he's still alive maybe. Not if he were dead.'

Julie-Anne stared at him.

'What do you mean?'

'Just this. I can implicate nobody but Tony, but who can Tony implicate? Someone tried to drown me, and it wasn't him. No, it's no good – I couldn't promise him, but I wish to heaven he hadn't asked…however that unfortunate man died, there's a would-be murderer on the loose. I couldn't do it…could I?'

Julie-Anne shook her head. 'No, I see that. You could have when you weren't sure, but you couldn't possibly now.'

'Thank you,' said Merlin. Julie-Anne looked at him.

'What will you do?'

'Go to the police about it, I suppose. At least if I do that, the worst, may not happen to Tony. I can't do anything else for him.'

'He was terrified,' said Julie-Anne soberly. 'I think you should do it soon. Shall I telephone for you?'

'No. I'm going to get up. You can get the car out while I get dressed in something warmer if you would.'

'Oh no,' said Julie-Anne. 'You're not going out in this weather – you've just had pneumonia, or its first cousin! Don't be a fool!'

'You won't have much success stopping me,' said Merlin, throwing back the bedclothes and pushing her off the bed. 'It's you that's the fool. Telephone them, and how soon do you think they'll get here? It's quicker by far to go to them. I don't want his blood on my head. Now go and get the car out, and don't argue – '

Julie-Anne opened her mouth to do just that, but a knock at the door interrupted her. Mrs Bartle came in.

'Dr Finn,' she announced.

VIII

'Murder most foul, as in the best it is;
But this most foul, strange and unnatural.'
Shakespeare: Hamlet

He was in the room even as Mrs Bartle spoke; there was no time for Julie-Anne to say anything, not even as much as the briefest warning, nor, once he was there, could she think of any cunning innuendo to convey a caution. She had to go downstairs with Mrs Bartle and hope that her suspicions of the young doctor were unfounded or else, at worst, that Merlin would think that the police, and the police alone, were the proper recipients of any information.

As on another occasion, she sat on the hall table, but this time she was alone. There was no sign of Austine. She sat there for what seemed like a very long time, until her strained imagination began to picture Merlin being murdered by the doctor upstairs in the big, dark, room, in some fiendish way known only to doctors, that would leave no mark...*natural causes,* for instance. Twice, she was half off the table, ready to run upstairs and rescue him, until common-sense reasserted itself. However villainous, the worst that Dr Finn was likely to do to Merlin here was knock him out temporarily with something, and there was no point that she could see in doing so. It must be obvious that other people besides Merlin himself would know the story of that fatal night and with no way of telling whom they might be, only an idiot would add fuel to the flames.

They would have to stop the story spreading somehow. Whoever 'they' were...Tony had just about had time to tell the doctor of the failure of his appeal to Merlin's better nature. It wouldn't be left there, surely? Her heart began to thump unevenly. To arrive so promptly, Dr Finn must have been waiting very near the house. It was uncommonly nasty to think about. She found herself wishing passionately for the company of Sylvester.

It felt like an age, but must have been, in reality, about twenty minutes, before Dr Finn came downstairs again. He looked cheerful, and was humming to himself as he reached the hall.

'Hallo there,' he said. 'You know, I think that guardian of yours is going to survive in spite of me. Not really fit to travel yet, but I think you might risk it if you take care. Make him wrap up well.' He headed towards the door, as Julie-Anne slipped off the table. 'Don't trouble, I'll see myself out. Have a safe journey.'

The door banged behind him. Julie-Anne stood in the cold, stone-flagged hall and stared at it after he had gone. The way was officially cleared for their departure, all that now remained was for pressure to be applied to make certain that they really did depart. She found she was actually beginning to feel physically sick with the strain; people with the stomach for the act of mutilation described by Merlin were not going to play games, and she was shakenly aware that they had not only to silence Merlin, but also to make him, in his turn, silence an indeterminate number of unknown people to whom he might have talked. They could not – thank goodness –possibly know that it was only herself and Sylvester that they had to worry about.

Ten minutes later, Merlin joined her in the hall, fully dressed to go out He had obviously not changed his mind about going to the police himself, but Julie-Anne was pleased to see that he had at least had the sense to put on a thick sweater, and had his sheepskin coat slung over his shoulder. He looked ill, and sounded worse, but his decision was manifestly unshaken.

'I waited,' said Julie-Anne, adding baldly, 'I was afraid to go outside on my own.'

'Afraid?' asked Merlin, pausing at the foot of the stairs. 'What of?'

'The doctor, I think,' said Julie-Anne.

'Finn? Why on earth?'

'He said something – that day he came when you were so ill. He made me think he had something to do with it all.'

'What did he say?'

'Nothing you could put your finger on, really. It seemed so silly, that in the end I didn't even mention it to Sylvester. But I didn't forget it, and then he came so quickly after Mr Manners – 'She broke off abruptly, as the telephone began to ring on its table in the corner. So strung up was she that she literally jumped. Merlin threw his coat on to the table and went to pick up the telephone, raising an eyebrow at her as he went past.

'You are in a bad way,' he observed, and lifted the receiver. 'Hello?' He was still half-laughing at her as he spoke, but a moment later the laugh was gone from his face. 'Wait a minute –' he said, and then slowly put the receiver back on its rest. He had turned a little pale.

'Who was it?' asked Julie-Anne.

'I don't know…' said Merlin, slowly. 'He asked for me, but he didn't wait. He just said, "Go and look in the moat. I'll ring back in ten minutes." Then he just rang off.'

Julie-Anne gulped. 'What did he mean?'

'I haven't the faintest idea, I'm just going to see.'

'Wait – ' cried Julie-Anne, as he made for the door. 'You've forgotten your coat – ' Her cry fell on deaf ears, and she ran after him, herself remembering neither his coat nor her own.

The moat ran round two sides of the house; to the right, as one came out of the front door, it started in the shrubbery and ran in an L-shape close to the wall of the house down the side and along the back. At the far end of the house, it narrowed to a ditch which ultimately ran into the drain. At the nearer end, where the water was much overhung with dense laurels and other shrubs, Merlin had paused. He stood very still, looking down; as Julie-Anne came up to him she saw why. A man was floating face downwards in the dark water, waterlogged and half-dragged under by the weight of his wet outdoor clothing. It was obvious that there was no hurry about getting him out.

Merlin spoke without looking round; his raised right hand clutched an overhanging branch, and the knuckles were white.

'Find Bartle,' he said. Julie-Anne hesitated, staring appalled at the thing in the moat.

'It's Mr Manners,' she said, uselessly.

'Go quickly,' said Merlin, and as she turned to run he was already kneeling on the bank, reaching for the body of his friend to haul it ashore.

'Just don't you dare to slip,' said Julie-Anne, and raced back along the drive to the house.

Bartle was in the kitchen; he dropped what he was doing and came at once when Julie-Anne told him what had happened.

'You stop here with me and have a nice cup of tea,' said Mrs Bartle, when Julie-Anne made to follow him. 'Frozen you be, and shocked too. Bartle and Mr Merlin will manage.'

'No, thank you,' said Julie-Anne. 'I'm all right – they might need a hand.' She did not want to stay in the kitchen with Mrs Bartle, answering questions, but she got no farther than the hall. The telephone, black and silent, sat on its little table in the corner. The seconds ticked slowly by. When it finally did ring, she pounced on it before it could give more than a preliminary 'brrr'.

'Hello, Raven's Dyke,' she said breathlessly.

'Mr Ravenscourt, please,' said the voice on the other end.

'He's busy.'

'I'll wait,' said the voice, in the tone of one who has all the time in the world.

Julie-Anne went reluctantly outside again. Merlin and Bartle had brought Tony Manners' body ashore, and were uselessly engaged in trying to revive him.

'The telephone,' she said. Merlin sat back on his heels.

'It's no good anyway,' he said. 'Stay with him, Bartle, will you? I'll phone the doctor, or the police, or someone. I won't be long.'

'He gave you more than ten minutes,' said Julie-Anne, as they walked together back to the house. Merlin did not answer; he was pale, with a tense, shut look about his expression that precluded further speech.

In the hall, he picked up the telephone, and motioned to Julie-Anne to come close enough to hear what was said.

'Ravenscourt here.'

'Ah,' said the voice on the other end. 'You've found our little surprise, I imagine? No – say nothing. Listen. You were drunk that night, and slipped off the bridge. Remember that, please. We have another little surprise for you, to help you to forget the rest. I'll telephone this evening – and remember, you wouldn't like to find one of your pretty wards in the moat, would you?' There was a click, followed by emptiness. Merlin put the receiver back.

'I don't like their surprises,' said Julie-Anne, uneasily.

'Where's Austine?' asked Merlin.

'Austine?' said Julie-Anne, and realized that she had not seen her sister since breakfast. 'I don't know. I haven't seen her. Merlin – you don't think…?'

She was closer to him that she had ever been before, but no thought of her fresh, newly-born love for him came to her mind, caught as it was in the grip of a new and horrible fear.

'Go see if you can find her,' said Merlin, urgently, picking up the telephone again. 'I'll come and help you as soon as I've phoned the police. Hurry.'

Julie-Anne ran swiftly through the house, opening doors, looking into rooms, calling her sister's name, but there was no reply. Austine's outdoor coat hung in the wardrobe, her outdoor shoes sat neatly under the bed, but if she was in the house then she was deliberately hiding, and that was so unlikely as to be ridiculous. Julie-Anne even knocked on Sir Richard's study door, and asked him if he had seen Austine, or knew where she was, but he had no knowledge of her. Nor had Mrs Bartle, recruiting her strength with strong tea in the kitchen after the shock of learning about the tragedy in the moat. She met up with Merlin again in the hall.

'No sign of her,' she said. 'What shall we do?'

They went into the living room and sat down by the fire.

'Did you phone the police?' asked Julie-Anne, unnecessarily, to set the conversational ball rolling.

'Yes. They're bringing a doctor out with them.'

'Did you say he was murdered?'

'Well, was he?'

'Merlin,' said Julie-Anne. 'Are you going to tell them? About…well, are you going to tell them?'

Merlin passed a hand across his face in a nervous gesture; he looked terrible.

'At this moment, I don't know what to do,' he admitted. 'On the whole, I think not – don't you?'

'Oh, thank goodness!' cried Julie-Anne in heartfelt relief.

'You see,' said Merlin, half to himself, 'if we don't know yet, officially, I don't have to decide, do I? I mean, about the other night. If they say nothing, the police that is, I don't have to either – yet.'

'They'll want to know why Tony Manners was here this morning.'

'Enquiring about my health?'

'Mrs Bartle will tell them that he was in a state when he arrived, because he was. Ranting around all over the place, saying he must see you.'

'She can be a very irritating woman. Perhaps she irritated him.'

'To the point of suicide?'

'Suicide?'

'Well, he didn't fall in by mistake, did he? And if he didn't come about what he did come about – if you see what I mean – '

'I think so,' said Merlin.

'Yes, well, in that case, he must have thrown himself in on purpose.'

'Who knows what he did? We don't, and that at least is true. He could have gone over to look at the water level; under the circumstances that could have been considered natural. It may even be no more than the truth. He went over to look, slipped, and was overcome by the cold and the weight of his overcoat before he could climb out again.'

They fell silent for a minute.

'And Austine?' asked Julie-Anne.

'She may have just slipped out for a walk,' said Merlin, but not as if he believed it.

'On a beastly cold, wet morning with just her slippers and no coat? Oh, Merlin!'

'I know, I know, but what would you have me do about it? I'm as much in the dark about what's going on as you are. I just wish I'd made you go back with Sylvester, and then you couldn't have been mixed up in it.'

'Merlin – '

'Tony's dead, thanks to me, and Austine probably kidnapped, and I'm being blackmailed into hiding a serious crime – how do you think I feel?'

'What are we going to do?' asked Julie-Anne, coming full circle.

He did not answer her, but sat staring unseeingly into the fire. After a minute or two, she tried again.

'Oughtn't you to tell your father about having a drowned man in his moat?' Some of the anger and anxiety she felt over Austine came out in her voice; even to herself it sounded catty and hateful. Merlin jerked round to look at her. Her eyes met his for a moment, but she could read nothing in them, dark and grey and expressionless. He got to his feet.

'You're right, of course,' he said, and walked out of the room.

Left alone, Julie-Anne felt a strong inclination to burst into tears, but reflecting that it would do no good to anyone, she fought it back. It came to her, queerly, that much as she loved him, she did not know Merlin well enough even to be sure she could lean on his judgement. She knew nothing about him at all, in fact, except that her step-father had trusted him and that her own heart was, without rhyme or reason, at his feet. Living as they had been for the last fortnight, they were in limbo, a little community entirely sufficient unto itself, the rest of the world cut off and forgotten. Now the world was about to overwhelm their isolation, and against the background of wider events, they would all appear to each other as different people. As things stood, it would be a testing time indeed – and if she, Julie-Anne, carried on as she had just been doing, she was not going to come out of the test with very high marks. Austine was her sister, but the responsibility for her was Merlin's, and she would do better to try and help him rather than scratch at him. He had been quite seriously ill, and was now confronted with an appalling situation, and there was only herself in a position to help him, so what did she do? Knowing this, and knowing too that there was competition in the romantic field, she took the first opportunity that offered to rip up at him like a shrew.

'Fool!' said Julie-Anne to herself.

Merlin did not come back to her, not surprisingly, and after a while, hearing the doorbell, and the sound of voices at the door, Julie-Anne got up and went out into the hall. Merlin, Sir Richard and two policemen were standing by the table, and a panda car was parked in the drive. Julie-Anne went to stand beside Merlin and, without looking at her, he reached out and drew her to him, his arm around her shoulders. She could not flatter herself that the gesture was more than brotherly, but at least it was friendly, and a little comforting.

The policemen had brought out a doctor with them (not Dr Finn, much to Julie-Anne's relief), and a photographer. Statements were taken from the household as to how Tony Manners came to be on the premises, and the finding of the body, and then the last remains of the late landlord of the Lamb and Flag were put into an ambulance and driven away down the watery lanes to the mortuary at Lowestoft, and the policemen got back into their car and drove away. Austine's continued absence had, of course, been remarked, and the police left a message that she was to contact them on her return from her walk. The whole incident seemed to have slipped by as smoothly as water down the river, but a curious unease remained when the household was alone once more. Sir Richard, shutting himself firmly back into his study, found it difficult to concentrate on his work, and the Bartles, down in the kitchen preparing what was going to be an extremely late lunch, talked excitedly; nothing so out-of-the-way had happened at Raven's Dyke for years. Julie-Anne and Merlin went back to the living-room fire.

'Austine hasn't come back,' said Julie-Anne, miserably.

'No,' said Merlin. 'Did you really expect it?'

Julie-Anne shook her head, unable to speak past a lump in her throat. He pushed her into a chair by the fire and sat on the arm beside her: she leaned her cheek against the comfort of his warm, woolly sweater and for the second time that morning, took a firm hold on herself. Hysterics would be no more helpful than snarling had been, and Merlin had enough to worry about as it was. She looked up at him, with a pitiful attempt at a smile.

'What can we do' she asked, shakily.

'That's a very good question, but I can't find a very good answer to it. Nothing?'

'Oh, Merlin…'

'Until the mystery voice calls us this evening, we've no idea what's expected of us, even, beyond a convenient blank in my memory, and they're welcome to that if Austine is safe.'

But supposing the police get poking around? They weren't happy.'

'You thought that, too, did you? That makes two of us…'

'Perhaps they found a clue. Maybe…had he…had he been hit or…or anything? Did you see, when you got him out? He wasn't…' Her voice trailed off uncertainly, and Merlin answered her with firmness.

'He was quite undamaged so far as I could see, so stop giving yourself horrors, young Julie-Anne.'

'Austine must be so frightened,' said Julie-Anne, shooting off at a tangent.

'There's nothing we can do about that. When there is, we'll do it. They aren't going to hurt her you know. They're using her as a weapon to blackmail me. I've got to pay up.'

'Can you? You know your friend was murdered, even if the police aren't sure of it.'

'He's dead. Austine is alive, and she's going to stay that way.'

'But – '

'We can only take it as it comes until we know a bit more. Whatever Tony was mixed up in, he must have counted the risks. Austine wasn't given the option. That's all that counts at present.'

'Suppose…just suppose that you found out what it was, and it was something you couldn't condone…s-smug druggling, or something?'

The inherent disaster of the situation and Julie-Anne's ridiculous mistake caught Merlin off balance, and quite without meaning to, he burst out laughing.

'It's not funny!' cried Julie-Anne, and to her own horror, found herself crying. Merlin, who already felt the end of the situation slipping out of his grasp, gathered her into his arms and held her close, with a look of despair at the opposite wall – which, naturally enough, gave no counsel.

'I'm sorry,' he said, stroking her hair soothingly. 'I didn't mean to laugh, it was just the way you said it. I'm sorry…'

'I'm s-s-sorry, too,' sobbed Julie-Anne, and yielding to circumstances, abandoned herself to the unaccustomed luxury of a good cry.

'Feel better now?' asked Merlin, when she had finished. Julie-Anne, her head leaning against his chest, gave a watery sniff.

'Your heart is going like a steam-engine,' she informed him. 'A rather wheezy steam-engine. You should be in bed.'

'Never mind me. Are you all right now?'

She nodded and drew herself away from him, mopping her wet face with an inadequate handkerchief. A hero of romance would immediately have offered her a perfectly laundered, masculine square, but Merlin merely remarked, 'It's no use you borrowing mine – it's unfit, like me. Go up and wash your face, you'll feel better. I'll let the police know about that call, and then I'll be up too – go in by my fire and I'll join you there.'

On the whole, Julie-Anne reflected as she made her way up to her room, she was glad to get away. Pleasant as it had been to be held in Merlin's arms, it was hardly the moment for a romantic interlude, even had romance been present, and she could not kid herself that it had been.

'He's going to be a brother to you,' Julie-Anne told her reflection. 'When he's finished being a father, that is. You may as well make up your mind to it, my girl, you're on a level with Austine,' And then remembering what had happened, 'Oh, Tina, where are you?'

Where indeed?

The day passed slowly. Sir Richard did not appear to notice Austine's absence from the lunch table, but even he was unlikely to overlook it at the dinner table, and Merlin and Julie-Anne spent some time during the afternoon trying to think up a suitable story to account for it.

'It's no good,' said Julie-Anne, at last. 'Everything we say sounds sillier than the thing before, and your father is nobody's fool.'

'True,' agreed Merlin. 'But he's also too courteous to call us a pair of arrant liars, so we'll adopt the least unlikely of our tarradiddles, and say she caught the bus into Lowestoft this morning and couldn't get back because of the floods.'

'Did the bus run to Lowestoft this morning?'

'I haven't the faintest idea, but nor will my father have.'

Had it not been so deadly serious, Julie-Anne thought, it would have had its amusing side. The question she had asked that morning had not been answered, nor did she feel she wanted to refer to it again. She longed for the evening to come, when at least something would inevitably happen.

It was a long time before anything did, however. Sir Richard, accepting without comment the explanation offered him for Austine's non-appearance at the dinner table, appeared not to notice that the two members of the party who were present were totally off their food and preoccupied to the point of being distrait. He alluded once to the 'unfortunate occurrence' of the morning, received no response, and withdrew into his normal thoughtful silence. It was impossible to decide whether he was aware of under-currents or no, but his two companions were grateful for his apparent self-absorption, pushing their food round their plates and thankfully giving up any pretence at either eating or conversation.

The telephone sat quietly in its corner, out in the hall.

After dinner was over, Sir Richard bade his son and his son's ward a courteous good night, and withdrew to his own fastness. Merlin and Julie-Anne went back into the living room. Merlin by this time was looking like death, and Julie-Anne had a strained appearance that had added five years to her age. They had little to say to each other, Julie-Anne merely remarking:

'Do you think he noticed anything wrong?' of Sir Richard. Merlin shrugged his shoulders.

'After a lifetime of being careful not to notice things, he's hardly going to start now,' he said. There was a faint bitterness in the observation which reminded Julie-Anne of the life he must have led, casually abandoned here and there by Anabel, and to all intents and purposes ignored by Sir Richard. Merlin must have learned early in life to paddle his own canoe; perhaps he would know enough to keep them all afloat now.

The evening dragged by like an eternity. Julie-Anne fidgeted round the room picking things up and putting them down again, sitting down, getting up, taking another turn around the room. Merlin sat slumped in an arm-chair and watched her. The only sound that either of them made for what seemed like a hundred years was the click and rustle of Julie-Anne's maddening gyrations, and an occasional burst of unhealthy-sounding coughing from Merlin. By the time the telephone finally rang at ten o'clock, they had quietly driven each other to the point of madness, but neither of them had the heart to say so.

'There it is!' said Julie-Anne, and leapt for the door, colliding heavily with Merlin on the way, for he had sprung to life like a released spring at the first ring.

The same voice as before spoke to them.

'One moment, I have a message for you.' There was a click, and a whirring noise, and then Austine's voice spoke, slightly distorted by what was obviously a recording.

'This is Austine here. I'm quite all right…' The voice faltered a little, and picked up again. 'I shall be quite safe as long as you do as they say. You know what that means. They say you know…please do as they say… or I may never see you again.'

'You heard that,' said the voice. 'Now listen, and do exactly what you are told. Make any excuses you feel are necessary to your other ward, and return home tomorrow. The unfortunate accident to your friend won't stop you. We shall contact you there in due course. Good night to you, Mr Ravenscourt – and sleep well.'

There was silence. Julie-Anne took the telephone from Merlin's hand, and replaced it on its rest. Now that she had heard Austine's voice, and there was no possibility of error, she found that she felt perfectly calm. There was a lot to be said for knowing the worst; bad times might come yet, probably would but the frightful uncertainty of the last few hours was over.

'Come on,' she said, gently. 'I've said it before, I know, but you should be in bed. Tomorrow is also a day.'

Merlin caught her hands, and held them. 'Julie-Anne, how can I say

I'm sorry? You know I wouldn't have had anything like this happen for the world.'

'I should be very foolish if I didn't,' said Julie-Anne. 'There's nothing you can do now. Tomorrow, we'll do as we're told. Now, for goodness' sakes, stop the dramatics and go to bed, before you drop!'

There was after all quite a bit of Anabel in him, she reflected, as she prepared herself for bed in her lonely room. Looks, undeniably, and that trick of developing the full drama of a given situation, which, exploited to the full by the woman, was, she thought, unconscious in the man. But he had an integrity that was completely lacking in his lovely mother, and that was what might prove Austine's undoing – or his own. Should he find himself forced into the position of deciding between risk to Austine and covering up for some even greater crime, the resultant decision, whichever way he decided, would leave a deep and fearful mark that neither time nor future events would serve to heal, unless something very unexpected indeed happened meanwhile.

Julie-Anne put out the light and climbed into bed, where she lay on her back watching the fire shadows flickering on the ceiling. She wondered where Austine was and then tried to shut out the speculation, it had too many avenues to explore.

Merlin, like his father, was no fool. He was, she knew, as well aware as herself of the choice that lay before him. Knowledge of the exact nature of the crime he was asked to condone would not, in the final analysis, make that much difference, its character was inherent in the price that was asked for his silence. She felt a great thankfulness, paradoxically, of her certainty that he did not love her, that she could not weigh in the scales on either side. She need have no part in the choice that he must make, except to stand by his ultimate decision.

But that wasn't true, was it? Julie-Anne sat up, and hugged her knees. Her own love for him had come upon her as suddenly as a summer storm, but she knew that there was nothing transient in it. That being the case, how could she stand aloof and watch him dash himself to pieces on the reef of circumstances beyond his control? Pure accident had brought him into this, not any volition of his own.

'So you can't be the what's-its-name, and pass by on the other side,' she told herself, firmly. 'If he falls flat on his face over this, you fall with him, and you know it.'

She lay back again, and began to think, wide-eyed in the dimness, as the fire died slowly back to red embers and the wind rattled the window frames, reminding, always reminding, of the crime it had uncovered.

It was going to be a very long night.

IX

*'O what a tangled web we weave,
When first we practise to deceive!'*
                    Sir Walter Scott: *Marmion*

The body in the river and its counterpart in the moat were of some concern to other people besides those at Raven's Dyke. The afternoon that had passed so interminably for Merlin Ravenscourt and Julie-Anne Austin had been full of problems for the police, too.

'Not a very nice case,' said Superintendent Gardner, of the local CID. 'I should be happy to think it wasn't mine. Do you think he really was Big Mick Carruthers?'

The two men in blue overalls and ex-naval duffel-coats who sat opposite him exchanged a glance.

'Who can tell for certain?' said one. 'No face, no fingerprints, no distinguishing marks – someone is very clever, but he has a nasty mind, but then, drugs is a nasty business. The post-mortem may throw up some information.'

'Right build, right colouring,' said the second man. 'But how many portly, grey-haired, middle-aged men do you know?'

The Superintendent, who answered that description fairly well himself, nodded sadly.

'We can make an educated guess,' continued the second man. 'Sergeant Willett here traced him as far as Ipswich, and our information is that he was heading this way. What I can't make out, is how the people this end drummed up the courage to bump him off. I mean to say, Mr Big himself – they must know they can't get away with it. If we don't get them, their own side will.'

Superintendent Gardner shuffled the papers on his desk together and spread them out again.

'We've been watching our end pretty closely, and nobody seems to be doing anything they shouldn't. Are you sure the stuff was coming in around here?'

'Positive.' Sergeant Willett rose to his feet and went over to a map pinned to the wall. He put his finger on a certain spot.

'Information goes that the thing was worked from here,' he said. 'Whytham St Giles – that's where we're putting up. No names, beyond the name of the village itself. There's a lot of private craft lie in the Whythe in the summer, mainly belonging to pillars of local society, and equally reputable people who come down from town for the weekend. It's a job sifting through them all, and so far they all seem to be above suspicion. And if our faceless friend is Big Mick, that hangs together, for our informant said he was getting out by the same route as the merchandise gets in.'

'Most of the craft are laid up at this time of year,' observed the Superintendent. 'That narrows the field.'

'Not as much as you might think.' The Sergeant's finger ran northwards up the coast. 'Here we have Lowestoft, Great Yarmouth, the Broads – all places where boats can lie safely all winter long if need be. Many of the bigger craft do, and it's the big craft we're looking for. Folk that ply far afield in the summer months, and take the odd trip in the winter time. When this country got too hot for him, Big Mick was planning a yachting expedition, there's little doubt about that. But he ended up – if so be it is him – rather shop-soiled at the bottom of the River Whythe. Someone round here must be barmy!'

'It certainly seems like it.' The Superintendent turned to the other man. 'What's your feeling, Inspector?'

'They needn't be as barmy as all that,' said Inspector Grey, thoughtfully. 'Carruthers didn't believe in letting his right hand know what his left was up to. Nobody seems to know, even among his own men, who was in charge down here. Probably lucky for him.'

'But with Mick Carruthers dead, he's killed his trade, whoever he is,' objected the superintendent. 'He daren't get in touch with Big Mick's people; even anyone else would be a risk.'

'Maybe he feels that's not too high a price for the privilege of going on living?' suggested the inspector.

'Once it gets out that Big Mick's dead he'll have to watch his Ps and Qs a bit,' said the Sergeant. 'One false move, and heaven help him!'

'Didn't you pick up any leads at all?' asked the Superintendent, adding apologetically: 'Perhaps I shouldn't have asked.'

'Not at all,' said Grey. 'We only had one vague idea – and you'll probably laugh like a drain if we tell you that one.'

'Try me,' said the Superintendent.

'Well, we did wonder about the landlord of our pub,' said Inspector Grey, half-apologetically. 'He seems to have lived here for ever, and to have led a blameless life, but there was one slightly fishy story we turned up about him, although we haven't had a chance to check it yet – '

'The landlord of your pub?' said the Superintendent, sitting up suddenly. 'The pub at Whytham? The Lamb and Flag? Tony Manners, you mean?'

'I said you'd laugh,' said the inspector.

'I'm not laughing,' Superintendent Gardner pulled his lower lip thoughtfully. 'Tony Manners was found dead this morning – floating in the moat at Raven's Dyke.'

Both his hearers became instantly alert.

'Raven's Dyke – that's the big house out on the road to Southwold?' said the Inspector. 'Sir Richard Ravencourt's place?'

'That's it – it was Sir Richard's son that found him. Accident, apparently. He'd been visiting there.'

Inspector and Sergeant exchanged a glance again.

'This fishy story we heard,' said Inspector Grey. 'It wasn't precisely unconnected with Sir Richard's son. Can you fill me in on the details of this – accident?'

The Superintendent told them what he knew.

'I can let you have copies of the statements if you like,' he added. 'They don't amount to much. It appears that Ravenscourt had an accident himself a week or so ago, and Manners just about saved his life. He's been ill since, and Manners called to see how he was getting along. Which is reasonable on the face of it.'

'On the face of it?'

'Well, there was one odd thing. The housekeeper apparently stressed that Manners was in a rare taking over something – but she's one of those that like a sensation, from all accounts, and we didn't take much heed.'

'In a rare taking over this Ravenscourt?'

'Yes. Demanded to see him, said it was important, that sort of thing.'

'This Ravenscourt,' said Inspector Grey, thoughtfully. 'He's always cropping up. Does he live with his father?'

'No. Doesn't live round here at all, if that's what you're getting at, nor own a boat round here. He lives down in Dorset at the principal family seat. He used to manage the estate in the old lord's time, but I heard that this new Lord prefers to handle things himself since he came of age, and Ravenscourt – who's a first cousin – has gone into business with a friend.'

'Doing what, in particular?'

'Building boats.'

'Boats again. Well, well.' The Inspector looked thoughtful. 'It seems a far cry from estate management.'

'I don't think he trained in estate management – came to it by accident, you might say,' said the Superintendent, with the comfortable superiority engendered by his life-long knowledge of the local aristocracy. 'His mother was an actress, and flighty as bedamned, and he's knocked around a bit himself.'

'To the extent of getting mixed up in running drugs?' asked the Inspector, sharply. But this the Superintendent would not allow. Ravenscourt was a name to conjure with in this part of the world, and whatever he might think of flighty actresses, or their footloose offspring, he wouldn't hear a word against Sir Richard, or anyone connected with him, unless it came from his own lips. Certainly not from two Londoners who wouldn't know a Ravenscourt if they saw one.

'It's odd, though,' said the Inspector, frowning slightly. 'This fishy story about Manners I mentioned – that was about…what's his name?'

The Superintendent cleared his throat. 'Merlin,' he said, half-apologetically.

'Poor fellow,' said Inspector Grey, in passing. 'As I was saying that concerned Merlin Ravenscourt, and now there's Manners drowned in this Merlin's father's moat. You did say moat?'

The Superintendent nodded. 'What story was this?' he asked.

'We got it from the cleaner down at the Lamb and Flag,' said Grey. 'It seems that Merlin…Merlin?…Ravenscourt came into the pub one morning with some story about having been banged over the head and dumped in one of the drains. Manners insisted he'd been drunk, and had fallen in on his own. They argued a bit, and then agreed to differ. We mentioned it to Manners, and he said the two of them had been drinking after hours, and his friend was stoned out of his mind, so he followed him home to see him safe, saw him slip and fall, and fished him out. We haven't seen Ravenscourt, because apparently, however it happened, it did him a bit of no good – and one disadvantage of our sort of enquiry is that you can't go barging into people's homes demanding to see them when they're ill without a very good reason indeed.'

'I can't say I'd heard that story, but in view of what's happened now, it has its interesting side,' said the Superintendent. 'I can check it for you, if it'll help?'

'Leave it a while,' said Grey, after some thought. 'Let's wait and see what the post-mortem brings up – either post-mortem. I get the feeling that it's too much of a coincidence for there to be no connection, that two bodies should be found floating around so soon after one another, and this funny story attached to one of them.'

The telephone on the Superintendent's desk rang, and he picked it up. A brief conversation followed, consisting – on the Superintendent's part – mainly of incredulous grunts.

'Thanks, Doctor, I'll pass it on,' he ended, and turned to the two Londoners.

'Well there's a turn up for the book,' he said. 'That was the pathologist. He hasn't finished yet, but he says that as far as he can see the man in the river died from a heart attack. 'The other injuries were inflicted after death.'

'Mick took tablets for his heart,' said Sergeant Willett.

'Did he so? It looks as if you may be on to something.'

'Something – but what?' said the Inspector. 'Now a nice connection between him and the late Tony Manners would be great – but they're so careful, these people. And Manners is dead.'

The two men left shortly after, muttering artistically about police persecution of the innocent. The Superintendent's own CID Inspector watched them go thoughtfully.

'Catchment Board men, aren't they?' he asked. 'Do you think they had anything to do with the dumping of Manners in the moat?'

'Drug Squad down from London,' said the Superintendent. 'Come into my room a minute, George, I want a word.'

Inspector Maitland listened to what his superior officer had to say with knitted brows.

' "Curiouser and curiouser",' he quoted, at the finish.

'You went out with the panda to Raven's Dyke this morning, didn't you? What did you think of it all?'

'It was a funny sort of accident, but not impossible.' The inspector rubbed his chin thoughtfully. 'The housekeeper said some funny things, but she lives a dull life.'

'And Ravenscourt? How did he strike you?'

'Yes. Merlin John Roland Ravenscourt...he had something on his mind, certainly.'

'Murder?'

'Do you know, I don't think so? But his very wealthy ward was unaccountably missing, for no good reason that anybody produced.'

'And what do you deduce from that?'

George Maitland spread his hands and shrugged his shoulders. 'That she had gone for a walk? Who knows?'

'I think,' said the superintendent, after a pause, 'that we had better keep an eye on Raven's Dyke. See to it, will you, George?'

'Certainly, sir,' said Maitland.

When he had gone to see about putting a watch on Raven's Dyke, the Superintendent sat alone for some while. The burden of his thoughts was not reassuring. He was a local man, and deeply feudal in his outlook. Whoever had Big Mick Carruthers die on his hands was not a happy man at this moment, his gruesome attempt to hide the fact notwithstanding, and there was Merlin Ravenscourt, out at Raven's Dyke, finding bodies in moats and with something on his mind. The quandary of having a notorious gangster with powerful and unpleasant friends possessing nasty suspicious minds, drop dead at his feet? Or what?

The Superintendent, too, was not a happy man. After a while, as if against his will, he put out a hand and picked up the telephone on his desk.

'Get me Chief Inspector Finch of the Embridge CID, will you?' he asked. 'Embridge in Dorset...yes...thanks.' He replaced the receiver and sat in deep thought waiting for his call to come through.

X

*'I have caught
An everlasting cold; I have lost my voice
most irrecoverably.'*
　　　　　　　　John Webster: The White Devil

Julie-Anne spent a restless night, with little sleep, and was up early. The night had brought no counsel, she was still torn two ways; on the one hand, Merlin must surely feel, whatever he said, that what went for Tony Manners – and had led swiftly to his death – must also go for Austine. The same rules must apply. If he could not bring himself to lie – or not to tell the truth, which amounted to the same thing – to save his friend, then neither should he do it for his sister. That was the situation, in basic shades of black and white. In fact, there were various shades of grey to be considered, too, Tony, by his own actions, had been convicted of guilt, whereas Austine was innocent. Then, too, Merlin had tried to act quickly enough to save his friend; for Austine there was only the certainty that but one thing he could do would save her. There were no alternatives. Were there?

She had asked herself the question a hundred times during that endless night. Merlin had probably done the same. Kneeling on the window-seat, watching the dawn break over the waterlogged fields, she wondered if he, like herself, was awake, tortured with indecision, trying to make up his mind what was right. Suppose he decided against Austine, as from an unbiased standpoint, he probably should; would she go on loving him if because of that decision Austine died? If he kept to what he had said last night, and some other terrible thing happened as a result, would he, even if Austine was saved, be able to live with himself afterwards? Was anyone justified in ignoring the obvious, simply because they did not know it as a fact? "Smug druggling", she had said, and he had laughed, but it hadn't been funny and both of them had known it. The east coast of England, with its hidden creeks and harbours and long, desolate coastline, had always been a jumping-off point for smuggling of one kind or another, and the Continent was only a step away; in the present context drugs were an easy conclusion to reach, and beside that deadly merchandise more prosaic goods – gold watches or wines and spirits or the old-fashioned silks, laces and tobacco – assumed an everyday innocence. If only it was gold watches, if only they could be sure, then it wouldn't be so hard. It was not knowing that was the problem, just guessing in the dark. Drugs caused so much misery and suffering to so many people; Austine's death in comparison, if it served to curb such a trade, would be a small thing, except to herself and Merlin and the small circle of people around them.

But if she died, it wouldn't stop anything, the thing was too big, everyone knew that, and beside one person you knew and loved personally, all those faceless victims didn't seem real. Anyway, it needn't be drugs at all.

Faceless victims…

If it was drugs, was Austine's safety, or Merlin's for that matter, going to be guaranteed by his silence?

Julie-Anne had been over the ground so many times that she could bear it no longer; she slid off the window-seat and crept along the passage to Merlin's room. Her knock on the door went unanswered, and on opening it, she found the room empty. The state of the bed bore witness to the fact that he, like herself, had spent a miserable night, but he must have left it some time ago, for his fire was nearly out and the room was cold.

Not quite knowing what else to do, Julie-Anne went downstairs. Mrs Bartle, she knew, always banked up the living-room fire before retiring at night so that room, at least, would be warm – the rest of the house was icy cold. As she passed the tall landing window she could see the rain pouring relentlessly down, streaming along the paths and dripping off the gutters. Everywhere had a uniform grey look about it. Illogical as it was, Julie-Anne felt that things would have been easier to decide if only the rain would stop and the sun would come out.

The old grandfather clock in the hall struck the half-hour as she passed it. Half-past six. A full hour before anyone else was likely to be stirring. She stood in the stone-flagged hall and felt desolation flood over her;

a whole hour left to think in, and no means of knowing where Merlin had gone. And what use did thinking do, anyhow? Julie-Anne felt at that moment that she could sink no lower; this was it, the nadir, the darkest moment – but where was the dawn?

Even as the thought went through her mind, she heard the car; a big one, with a heavy engine, from the sound of it, coming up the drive. Merlin was her first thought, being no expert on car engines, and she ran to the window.

But it wasn't Merlin. It was a big Land Rover and the man who drove it was a stranger to her. Disappointment and a jolt of fear blurred her sight for a minute, and then she blinked and saw clearly. The door of the cab bore a sign-written legend in neat white letters:

CHASE & RAVENSCOURT
BOATBUILDERS
23 DOUGLAS ROAD
ALDMERE
DORSET

and then a post code and a telephone number below.

As Julie-Anne watched from the window, the driver opened his door and jumped out to the ground, and a second man came round from the far side. This one was no stranger; she had never thought she would be so glad to see Sylvester. She ran to the door and opened it. Sylvester took one look at her, and reached her in one bound; he would never mean to her what his cousin did, but there was no doubt that his arms were strong and reassuring, and his chest quite as convenient to cry on – only this time, she wasn't going to cry! Oh no!

'I knew you'd all get into a mess without me,' said Sylvester, characteristically. 'As soon as I saw the evening paper, I knew it – didn't I say so?' he demanded over his shoulder.

'You did,' agreed his companion, and Julie-Anne recognized the pleasant country voice she had heard on the telephone.

'Come in out of the rain, it's no warmer indoors but at least it's relatively dry.' Sylvester transferred Julie-Anne from his chest to his left shoulder and led the way inside. 'Strewth! It's colder than I remember, if that's possible! Where's the nearest fire?'

'Probably the living room,' said Julie-Anne.

Sylvester, who seemed to carry about with him a heartening breath of optimism, strode across the hall and opened the living-room door. He paused.

'Good Lord, the ghost of Raven's Dyke walks again! What have you been doing to him, Julie-Anne?'

Julie-Anne, standing at his shoulder, saw past him to the arm-chair by the fire where Merlin lay asprawl, uneasily asleep, breathing roughly and unevenly. There was some justification for Sylvester's remark, for he looked ghastly. Sylvester looked at him for a moment, and then turned to look searchingly at Julie-Anne, then back to his cousin. He drew a deep breath.

'I get the feeling the laugh is on me after all,' he remarked. 'Can you tell us, Julie, or shall we wake up the sleeping beauty here?'

'I'll tell you,' said Julie-Anne. 'Leave him alone. I'll make some strong coffee for us all, and we can hold a council of war.' She turned to go away to do so, and encountered Sylvester's friend. He was looking at Merlin with a strange look in his eye. He was a smaller man than the two Ravenscourts, but wiry in build, with brown hair and eyes of a very deep, clear blue; sailor's eyes, thought Julie-Anne, liking him on sight. He had a tough, piratical air about him, which he was going to need if he proposed joining this party.

'Oh,' said Sylvester, remembering the social niceties. 'Sorry – I forgot that you and Robert are unacquainted. Julie-Anne, this is the Chase half of the partnership – Bob, this is Julie-Anne, who is not quite so beautiful as her sister but nevertheless, as you see, a considerable eyeful.'

'Fool!' said Julie-Anne. 'Hello, Bob. I'll go and make the coffee.'

When she returned from the kitchen with the tray she found that Sylvester had built up the fire to a roaring blaze, and that Merlin had woken up. Awake, he looked less ill, but unkempt and unshaven.

'Disreputable, in fact,' said Sylvester, eyeing him up and down. 'And you're not going to die quietly, are you? You look, and sound, like a consumptive tramp.'

'Thanks a lot,' said Merlin. 'Hello, Julie-Anne – couldn't you sleep, either?'

'Ugh!' said Julie-Anne, which everyone accepted as a fair comment on the night she had spent. Sylvester watched her pouring coffee with a measuring look.

'I take it,' he said, 'that the dismembered body spelled trouble for someone?'

'Yes. Me,' said Merlin.

'You could have knocked me down with a feather when I picked up the evening paper last night,' said Sylvester, soberly for him. 'I never quite believed you, you know. What did Tony have to say about it? Presumably he said something.'

'Not much, and he won't say any more. He's dead too' said Merlin.

There was a stillness in the room.

'Dead?' echoed Sylvester. 'How, dead? Did somebody kill him, too, or...?'

'I think I killed him,' said Merlin. Julie-Anne made a protesting movement, but a look from Bob stilled her.

'How?' he asked.

'He was killed, drowned in the moat as a matter of fact, because he saved my life.'

'You're a walking disaster area and no mistake, but I don't see that you can say that you killed him,' objected Sylvester.

'I wouldn't promise him silence,' said Merlin. 'So he's dead. And Austine is being held hostage for my future good behaviour.'

Sylvester jumped to his feet, suddenly white to the lips.

'Austine is! Where? Who by? For pity's sake, man, what's been happening here? What have you done?'

'He hasn't done anything, and sit down,' said Julie-Anne, sharply. 'Things are bad enough already, without you leaping about and shouting!'

Sylvester stood, biting his lip, and his colour crept slowly back. His eyes held a shocked look, but he had the grace to apologize.

'Sorry, Merlin,' he said. 'That took me by surprise.'

'What happened?' asked Bob Chase. 'Start at the beginning, and let's get it all straight. Julie-Anne can tell us – no, Merlin, you shut up! Drink your coffee, you look as if you need it, you can't die here.'

Julie-Anne smiled at him gratefully.

'You can tell who's the senior partner, can't you?' said Sylvester, who never deflated for long, it seemed. 'Now, Julie-Anne?'

Julie-Anne's account was brief, but accurate. A lot of it, Sylvester knew already, of course, but the events of the previous day were new to him, as were her suspicions of Dr Finn.

'There's no doubt, he does keep cropping up at every turn,' he agreed. 'But good heavens, Julie-Anne, it's natural enough. Merlin, here, has been lying at death's door, even I saw that. Finn was bound to be a recurring motif.'

'Yes, I know that,' said Julie-Anne. 'It wasn't his being here, it was what he said.'

'Womanly intuition?' queried Sylvester, raising his eyebrows.

'If you like.'

'I'm not sure that I do like. Still, he's the only clue we have, so I suppose we'll have to start with him. But how?'

'We can't start anywhere. We're to go home and shut up, not necessarily in that order – remember? If we don't Austine'll...Austine will be...'

Sylvester put a hand on her shoulder and gave it a comforting squeeze. 'No, she won't, because assuming that Dr Finn is the villain of this piece, he's going to know exactly why you didn't at the first opportunity.'

'How?' asked Julie-Anne, without hope but willing to be convinced. Sylvester looked at his cousin.

'Merlin looks very ill, don't you think?' he said. 'Much worse, in fact – it must be the shock, and splashing about in the moat yesterday. I really think you ought to call the doctor, Julie-Anne.'

There was a pause.

'That's clever,' said Bob.

'Sylvester, I really think you've got something,' said Julie-Anne. Sylvester looked smug.

'I'm not just a pretty face, you know. What do you think, cousin? You're very quiet.'

'You all told me to shut up,' said Merlin, 'and I'm quite all right, thank you very much.'

'You've got no imagination, that's your trouble,' observed Bob.

'You're Anabel's child,' Julie-Anne reminded him. 'Try and be like her – act, for once.'

'To achieve what?'

'To buy time,' said Sylvester. 'You'll have to act, too, Julie, that Finn is no fool. If Merlin said anything to anyone it's to you, or me, or Austine. You'll have to be half out of your mind, because on the one hand you've got this lout, my cousin, *in extremis*, and on the other, you have to get back to Ravenscourt Place to keep your bargain with the kidnappers. Bob and I'll keep out of the way somewhere, and as soon as he's here we'll damn well go and raid his house. If he's got Austine – '

Two interruptions occurred here.

'Who are you calling a burglar?' demanded Bob, startled, and Merlin returned to animation with a suddenness that made the others jump.

'No,' he said. 'Not the house.' He spoke so firmly that the other three didn't argue. Sylvester merely said:

'Not the house? Then where?'

Merlin turned to him. 'You know that place just down the coast from here – Thingummy's Quay – you know, where Boswell's yard is.'

'Smith's Quay,' said Sylvester. 'I know it.' He made a gesture to include Julie-Anne and Bob in the conversation. 'It's a nothing sort of place, out in the middle of nowhere, but no doubt he knows what he means unless he really is delirious, that is.'

'You shut your face,' said Merlin, who had had enough. 'Listen to me!'

Sylvester jumped to attention. 'Sir!'

Julie-Anne gave him a jab in the ribs with her elbow at the same instant as Bob caught him across the shin, and he subsided with a squawk of pain.

'Can't you be serious for two minutes together?' asked Merlin, angrily.

'It takes me that way,' said Sylvester. 'If I didn't place the fool, I'd tear the place apart…I'm sorry.'

'That's all right, but shut up, and stay shut up,' said Merlin, and Julie-Anne and Bob exchanged a pained glance.

'We'd got as far as Smith's Quay,' prompted Bob, diplomatically. 'What are we doing there?'

'Tony kept a boat there,' said Merlin. 'A big motor-cruiser. I haven't seen it, but he's shown me pictures. He and Finn, we're assuming, are hand in glove in whatever is going on, and if so, and ignoring fifty-six other unknown factors of course, it's a far more likely place to keep Austine hidden than his house, where his wife might ask awkward questions.'

'You can't half be nasty, when you try,' said Sylvester, but in a more subdued tone of voice. 'All right, we go there. How do we know when the coast is clear? Can Julie-Anne telephone somehow, or something, when Finn gets here?'

Merlin got up and went across to the window, and stood with his back to them watching the rain stream down the glass. 'The wind's dropping,' he observed.

Since that was quite obviously not what was on his mind, the others said nothing. After a moment, he said: 'I spent all night thinking…'

Julie-Anne bit her lip, and looked at his back. Her heart began to thump uncomfortably. This was it, then. The moment of trust, the reckoning time. How cool-headed was this man to whom she had given her heart, unasked? Would he take the risk, and gamble everything on the side of justice, or would he take the apparently safe way and play the crooked game? Half an hour ago, things had been different, but now a road, fraught with hazards, it was true, but still a road, lay between the two hard, the two impossible choices of Austine and absolute honesty. Sylvester was clever, Bob Chase was steady and strong, but Merlin? What was he? On impulse, she went over to the window beside him and slipped her hand in his.

'I was thinking, too' she said. 'You couldn't do it. It was no good saying you could.'

He looked down at her, and for that minute there might have been nobody else in the room.

'Will you ever forgive me if I turn out to be wrong?'

'Will it matter to you?' asked Julie-Anne.

It felt like an hour, but it must have only been a few seconds before he dropped her hand and turned away.

'All right,' he said. 'We'll try it. Julie-Anne and I will decoy Dr Finn, and you two can get down to Smith's Quay and take a look around – but don't let Sylvester do anything daft, Bob, will you, because we don't know that Finn hasn't half a dozen accomplices, should it be Finn we're after at all. And keep the Land Rover out of the way, with our name and address all over it. And as soon as you get clear of Whytham, stop and telephone the police, and get them out here...'

'He makes a wholesale performance of it once he gets started,' said Sylvester, admiringly. 'Well done, cousin; I thought for a moment there you were going to take the downhill path after all.'

'It'd just better go right, that's all,' said Merlin.

Sylvester got to his feet. 'Things being as they are, with great reluctance, I suppose we had better go before breakfast,' he said. 'Mrs B had better not set eyes on us, and you'd better take to your bed before she appears, too, Merlin – don't bother to shave, you look awful as you are. Take care of him, Julie. I'm not the only one that needs a keeper, he's hardly begun yet.'

When Sylvester and Bob had gone, Julie-Anne cleared the coffee cups on to the tray and took them down to the kitchen for washing. She had just dried the last one and hung it on its hook when Mrs Bartle appeared. She looked surprised to see Julie-Anne about so early.

'I let the fire go out, and I was cold,' said Julie-Anne, wondering how early she could decently discover Merlin at death's door.

'I'll make you a nice cup of tea,' said Mrs Bartle, bustling around.

Julie-Anne was already fairly full of coffee, but it occurred to her that she could turn the proffered tea to good account.

'That'll be nice,' she said. 'I could do with a cup. I'll take one up to Merlin, too – he's awake, I heard him coughing as I came downstairs.'

'You'll be wanting to get back south as soon as Miss Austine gets back,' said Mrs Bartle, busy with the kettle. 'We'll miss you all around the place; gave it a bit of life. I really think it's done Sir Richard good to have some young folk about for once. You'll be calling again, I hope?'

Julie-Anne thought that once she finally got away from Raven's Dyke, she would never want to see the place again, but she made some suitable reply, and escaped upstairs with her cups of tea.

Merlin was trying to relight his fire; he looked at the tea with disapprobation.

'Thanks for the thought, but no,' he said. 'Some kindling would be of more use – I shall freeze to death up here.'

'I'll get you some,' said Julie-Anne. She put the tray down on top of the chest of drawers and sat down on the bed.

'Merlin – I was thinking. Suppose the house is being watched?'

Merlin sat back on his heels and looked at her thoughtfully. 'You're not having second thoughts?' he asked. 'It's not too late to go back.'

'No, no, it's not that.' Julie-Anne rubbed her nose distressfully. 'I don't know what it is…perhaps I'm wrong, and it isn't Dr Finn at all. Oh, Merlin, what are we doing?'

'Taking a risk to save Austine,' said Merlin, slowly. 'It wasn't only that I didn't think it right to submit to being blackmailed, Julie-Anne…there was another reason why I couldn't just let nature take its course.'

'Yes, I know,' said Julie-Anne. 'I thought of it, too. How long have you to be quiet, and what happens to Austine whilst you're being it? What happens to you, come to that?'

'It's all so scrambled and amateurish,' said Merlin. 'Someone – Finn or anyone else – is just panicking in all directions and bumping off everyone in sight. Tony yesterday, Austine today, me tomorrow, you the day after – someone is being pursued by the hounds of hell, if you ask me, and I'd like Austine safe before they catch up with him.' He paused. 'He's already had a go at me, whoever he is – and a person whose answer to everything is a corpse isn't the sort of person I like my sister going around with.'

'That's one way of putting it, I suppose,' said Julie-Anne. She got off the bed. 'Well, I've had plenty of time to find you dying, so I suppose I'd better go and telephone Dr Finn. Merlin…what if it isn't him?'

'Oh, I think it is – beyond all reasonable doubt, that is, Him and Tony, and at least one other – and I rather think our homicidal maniac is the one other. With a bit of luck, Finn will take off from here and go straight to him, and the police can follow him. I get the feeling he hasn't far to go.'

Julie-Anne paused on her way to the door. 'Why, have you any idea who?'

'None at all – except that Boswell of Boswell's yard was another pal of Tony's, and he is a weirdo, if you like. Oh, no, I don't really know – we'll have to take it as it comes.'

Julie-Anne looked at him severely. 'I'm beginning to see what Sylvester meant about you,' she said: 'You really think this Smith's Quay place is it, then?'

'If it isn't then we'll have to start again, but it seems likely, doesn't it? All other things being equal, that is.' He paused. 'Julie-Anne…'

'What?'

'You and I, we've both got a lot at stake – stay with me, we'll beat them yet.'

'We must,' said Julie-Anne, and went downstairs to make her telephone call. It had occurred to her that Dr Finn might smell a rat, and when she had put the telephone down, she was only half sure that he had not. It was still early, and he had promised to call on his way to the surgery – in time, in fact, to make sure that if Merlin was fit to travel, he had time in which to do it. On the other hand, it could be a symptom of fear. She remembered Merlin's homicidal maniac, and hoped that he was right in thinking that it was some third person and not just indulging in wishful thinking. She went into the living room to wait for the doctor's arrival, and spent the time walking restlessly up and down. Worry about Austine, which had taken second place for a while, came back to the forefront of her mind. She wondered what Sylvester and Bob were doing, and how soon the police would get to Raven's Dyke. Not before Dr Finn had left, she feared. In which case…

She still had the keys of Merlin's car in her handbag. She fetched them, and went round to the garage and brought the car round to the front of the house, leaving it parked by the wall as if they were ready to load up and leave. When Dr Finn left, if the police weren't already here, someone else would have to follow him – and it looked as if it was going to have to be her. She was frightened, but she had courage.

She was hardly back in the hall before she heard the doctor's car in the drive, and as soon as she opened the door to him she knew that he was afraid, and not only afraid, but dangerous. His normal cheerful jocundity was missing, and there were beads of sweat on his forehead. She wished suddenly that it was still not too late to go back and hoped that Merlin would put up a performance worthy of his talented mother, because on what happened in the next few minutes a great deal depended – maybe even Austine's life. She was thankful, as she took the doctor upstairs, that there was no need for her to disguise her own uneasiness. 'Act', Sylvester had said – but if all she had to act was someone in the grip of searing anxiety, she could hardly go wrong!

It was as she was leaving Merlin's room to go downstairs that she heard the doorbell go. For a moment she did not realize its significance, and then, as the truth dawned on her, she felt her heart stop. She had thought of the police coming late, but not, surely not as early as this? Sylvester must have telephoned almost at once, but even so…it hardly seemed possible that they could come so promptly. Too promptly. They were going to run straight into Dr Finn, there would be no time for explanations, and no opportunity to follow him, and he…what would he think? What would he do?

There was one chance, and one chance only, and she lost it even as she ran to the head of the stairs. Mrs Bartle came running up to meet her and her voice, clear and carrying, must have been heard quite clearly by both Merlin and Dr Finn.

'Oh, Miss Austin – here's the police come asking for Mr Merlin, and the doctor here as I told them.'

'Thank you, Mrs Bartle, I'll speak to them,' said Julie-Anne. She was conscious of the woman at her elbow as she finished descending the stairs; poor Mrs Bartle, she meant so well but if only she had been quiet, if only she had left time enough to get the police concealed somewhere. Well, it was too late now.

Inspector Maitland came to meet her as she reached the stone flags. 'Good morning, Miss Austin, I believe we met yesterday?' He held out his hand. 'I'm sorry to disturb you so early, but I wanted to have a word with your guardian, isn't it? About Mr Manner's unfortunate accident yesterday.'

Julie-Anne stared at him, only half comprehending. 'But...didn't you get the message?' she asked.

'Message? What message?'

Of all the unfortunate chances, this must be the worst, thought Julie-Anne. Coming at just that moment, and not even sent for.

'Come in here,' she said, opening the living-room door. 'I'll explain – thank you, Mrs Bartle, I'll see to the inspector.'

Mrs Bartle looking affronted began to cross the hall towards the kitchen door, and Julie-Anne and Inspector Maitland were almost into the living room, when there was a sudden disturbance; a scuffle, a yell, the slam of a door and the sound of running feet. A second later, Dr Finn came flying down the stairs two at a time, and Merlin came hurtling behind him. The doctor vaulted over the table without bothering to go round it, and was through the front door like a bullet from a gun. The door slammed behind him, and Merlin crashed into it as it did so. The impact, which was considerable, appeared to daze him, and before he could get the door open again, the doctor's car was flying down the drive.

'Damn!' said Merlin, with feeling, and turned around.

Inspector Maitland cleared his throat cautiously. 'Trouble?' he suggested.

Merlin was looking decidedly queer. 'He just tried to kill me,' he said. 'When Mrs Bartle called out that the police were here...he came at me with a hypodermic and a murderous look...'

'He didn't get you, did he?' asked the inspector, hurrying around the table.

'Not all of it, just a bit...I don't know what it was, but I think it must have been quite lethal, because I'm beginning to feel most peculiar...'

'Merlin!' cried Julie-Anne, running forward. She was the last thing he saw before the flagged floor swung gently round to replace the wall, and darkness closed in.

XI

'O Captain! my Captain! our fearful trip is done,
The ship has weathered every rack, the prize we sought is won,
The post is near, the bells I hear, the people all exulting'
    Walt Whitman: O Captain! My Captain!

Smith's Quay lay about ten miles from Whytham St Giles, across the flooded fields It was an inlet, a small indentation in the shifting coastline, rather than a river, and therefore was not so subject to the ravages of floods. This much Sylvester was able to tell Bob as they drove swiftly along the water-skimmed roads. Beyond that fact, he knew very little about the place, as unlike his cousin he had never spent much time at Raven's Dyke; his uncle, Sir Richard, not being one who encouraged young nephews to visit. There was the boatyard there, rather seedy and rundown and doing barely enough trade to stay in business, which Merlin had mentioned, an old stone quay in the final stages of dereliction, from which the place derived its name, and a ramshackle jetty. Not one of England's beauty spots, said Sylvester, and just the place for a handy bit of skulduggery.

Bob answered him with a monosyllabic grunt, being fully occupied with driving on roads covered with a thin film of slimy mud. Away from the lands lying along the banks of the Whythe, the landscape, though sodden, was not under water but the relentless rain, still teeming down from the black heavens and lashed hither and thither by the battering winds, made driving treacherous and would have diverted his attention from Sylvester even had other considerations not done so. Bob had known both Ravenscourts long enough to know that, in some respects, there was not a pin to choose between them, and although he did at least have

Sylvester firmly under his eye, he was worried about Merlin: he did not think that Julie-Anne had fully taken his measure. On the surface, he knew from experience, the pair of them looked to outsiders as if they had little to say to each other, and less in common, but in fact they had a very good understanding of each other. The difference between them lay in the fact that while Sylvester thought of crazy things to do, Merlin found good reasons for doing them and generally bore the consequences, whilst his cousin, who appeared to bear a charmed life, managed to slide out from under. The basic sameness was that the crazy things were common to both, and neither was in the habit of totting up risks before he took them. 'Mad as a March hare,' Sylvester said of Merlin, and Merlin called Sylvester an idiot. Yes, definitely, they understood each other well.

When they reached it, Smith's Quay looked a long way from lively. Bob parked the give-away Land Rover by the side of the road, with its nose buried in scrub, and they had to trust to luck that nobody would look at it closely. With its back end turned towards the road, only the heavy towing bar gave any clue to its nautical origins, and that could equally indicate a farming background. They walked the remaining few hundred yards to Smith's Quay, their coat collars turned up against the rain and wind.

'Merlin said it was dropping,' grumbled Sylvester. 'They're all going to think we're crazy here, Bob; whoever would go for a walk in this weather?'

'There doesn't seem to be anybody around to think anything at all,' said Bob, adding, 'and I don't blame them. What a place!'

There appeared to be nothing at Smith's Quay except a couple of depressed-looking cottages and the boatyard, Boswell's Yard. This, too, looked depressed: a cluster of weathered and weary-looking sheds along the foreshore, with a few boats hauled up on to the shingle in front of them. The shed doors were all firmly closed and the whole place wore a shut-up look. A couple of yachts lay offshore to moorings, looking drab and cold, as yachts do in the wintertime when the rain is coming down; they tossed and yawed about uncomfortably on their chains, for even in the inlet the waters were choppy, and outside, beyond the sandbank that masked the entrance and made Smith's Quay a relatively safe all-the-year-round harbour, the sea could be seen, pounding in and breaking over the bank in clouds of flying spray.

'There's one thing,' said Bob to Sylvester, as they stood on the foreshore watching. 'He can't make a run for it by water. Look at that sea! You'd never get a boat through that harbour mouth today.'

Sylvester looked anxiously around him. 'That must be her,' he said, touching his friend's arm to call his attention. 'Look.'

A long wooden jetty ran out over the water, and a very few craft were tied to it: a shabby grey rowing-boat, a couple of dinghies and a big cruiser. The latter had all her windows covered with curtains (she was the sort of craft that definitely had windows, rather than portholes); she looked deserted, but there was no knowing. Bob and Sylvester, with apparent idleness, strolled along the jetty and stood there looking at her while the rain ran down their necks coldly.

'If that belonged to this Manners, he was well heeled,' remarked Bob. 'I wouldn't mind the money that little lot must have cost him.'

'He ran a Jag,' offered Sylvester.

'That pub of his...what was it called? Did it do a lot of business? I wouldn't have thought so, just there.'

'Not this sort,' said Sylvester. 'I don't like the smell of this, Robert, I don't like it at all. Shall we go aboard?' He made as if to do just that, but Bob's hand laid urgently on his arm made him pause.

'What's up?'

'We're about to have company,' said Bob. 'If ever you told a convincing lie, tell it now. Come on.'

A man was hurrying along the jetty towards them. He was big, with a broad, pale face and bright little eyes that missed nothing, and otherwise presented an extraordinary appearance, for the top of his head was completely bald, while the hair that grew luxuriantly round the sides was long and unkempt, and held back with an elastic band. Long hair for men is a controversial issue, but anyone would agree that there are those that can get away with it, and those that can't. It should have made him look ridiculous, but neither Bob nor Sylvester felt the slightest inclination to laugh.

'Hey!' he called, angrily. 'This is private property. You're trespassing.'

Sylvester put his hands in his pockets and tried to look casual. 'Sorry, we were just having a look around. That's a nice boat,' he nodded towards the big cruiser. 'My friend and I are looking for something like that. D'you build them?'

Boswell slowed down and looked at them measuringly, weighing the possibilities of a sale.

'No,' he said. 'Might do a deal, though. The owner has just died, and I reckon she'll be sold. Would you be interested?'

'We might be,' said Bob. 'Could we go aboard and look around, d'you think? Would anybody mind?'

'They might, or they might not, but I haven't the keys,' said Boswell. 'Got some details up in the office, I think.' Without waiting for a reply, he turned and began walking back along the jetty; Sylvester went with him, but Bob dawdled along behind, apparently taking another careful look at the cruiser. Boswell stopped, and waited for him. Sylvester thought he looked unhappy. Bob rejoined them.

'Sorry – was I keeping you waiting?'

They followed Boswell to his office, which overlooked the back of the yard, where there was a small parking lot with one or two cars and a few upturned boats in it.

'Been some nasty weather about,' said Boswell, as they went indoors out of the wind and rain. A gust sent the wooden building shuddering, and reminded them that there still was. 'Been bad some places. They had the floods out up the coast, I heard tell. Now then, let me see, where did I put the folder...?'

He began to rifle through a filing-cabinet and Bob and Sylvester, trying to look like eager customers, watched him and wondered about him.

'Walk, did you?' asked Boswell, without looking up. Sylvester sat up with a jerk, but Bob continued to lounge against the wall as if he hadn't a care in the world.

'No,' he said. 'We left the car up the road a bit. The road looked like a dead end back there, and we thought we'd walk on in case we couldn't turn. We wish we hadn't now.'

'Ah,' said Boswell. After some time, he found what he was looking for, and spread leaflets and photographs and catalogues over his desk. The three men pored over them, and Boswell did his best, they admitted afterwards, to sell Bob and Sylvester a boat that neither of them would have wanted even had they been able to afford her. Had they been concentrating harder, so said Sylvester, he might have done it, so persuasive was he. He was, in fact, in mid-flight when a car drove speedily into the yard, stopped in a flurry of gravel, and a man jumped out and came running towards the office. Sylvester drew back with an exclamation, but Boswell didn't appear to notice.

'Scuse me,' he said, pushing his way hurriedly past Bob and heading for the door. 'Won't be a minute – have a look whilst I'm gone, I won't be long – ' The door slammed behind him. Bob looked at Sylvester.

'Who?'

'Finn. Did you see his face?'

'Yes. Listen.'

There were sounds of violent argument outside the door, Boswell's voice once, shouting, 'You can't do it, I tell you – ' hurriedly lowered. The sounds of the two angry voices began to move away, and Sylvester and Bob were just about to follow when their attention was caught by the sight of two police cars sliding quietly into the car park.

'Come on,' said Sylvester, and made for the door.

They met a plain-clothes detective immediately outside.

'Mr Ravenscourt?' he asked. 'I was expecting to find you here. Anything happening?'

'Dr Finn just arrived,' said Sylvester. 'He's gone down to the jetty with the character that seems to run this place. They've got a boat, but they won't get away on it, the seas are too heavy – at least, they'd be fools to try.'

The detective waved on his companions. 'All right, lads. Take it quietly, he may be armed. Let's go get him.'

He didn't say anything to Sylvester and Bob, so they followed at a circumspect distance.

Boswell and Finn were out on the jetty by this time, and still arguing fiercely. Finn was bending over the mooring rope, frantically undoing it, and Boswell appeared to be trying to prevent him. Normally, he could probably have done so, but the young doctor was driven by desperation and they were both so engrossed that they never noticed the arrival of the police until they heard the thud of feet running along the jetty.

Boswell gave a yell of warning, and his hand flew to his hip; Finn took one look and leapt for the boat. The jetty was narrow, and Boswell a powerful fighter: by the time the first two policemen had been able to overpower him and the next one was able to get past, Finn had the engine running. The big cruiser began to reverse away from the jetty and the policeman sprang aboard. There was running and confusion, men shouting.

'He's getting away!' called someone, and someone else called, 'Don't shoot – you'll get Davies – ' Shots rang out and Boswell yelled something after his departing accomplice.

'Oh, God!' said Inspector Grey of the Drug Squad. 'Where does he think he's going?'

Sylvester watched as if frozen in a nightmare. 'He'll drown himself,' he said. 'Austine…' And then louder. 'Austine! She could be aboard! Do something somebody!' and he began to run uselessly along the jetty. The big cruiser was clear now, heading for the harbour entrance. The watchers on shore could see the policeman, Davies, backed against the cabin with his arms spread out, and Finn's back.

'He's got a gun,' said one of the others.

It was as if, for a minute, time had stopped. Nobody moved or spoke, and then Bob remarked to the inspector: 'What sort of seaman is your friend?'

'Rowboat on the Serpentine,' said Grey, bitterly. 'And Finn has a gun – here, where're you going?'

'Sailing!' called Bob, over his shoulder, and took off along the quay. Grey began to run after him, and then stopped. Sergeant Willett appeared beside him.

'We've got Boswell, anyway,' he said. 'Where's he off to?'

'I don't know…' said Grey. Sylvester answered him.

'He's got to come inshore at the end of the quay – look at the channel markers – that sandbank must come almost right across.' His voice was breathless, but flattened out of all expression.

'Hell – why didn't someone say?' cried Grey. 'Come on – '

There was a stampede along the quay, but although only moments had passed, Bob was too far ahead. Finn had not even seen him. The cruiser wallowed towards the end of the quay, and Bob, the impetus of his run behind him, leapt from the quay and the watchers saw him crash down on the foredeck. A moment later, the first of the seas caught the boat and swung her head over. Spray flew.

'Alert the lifeboat and the coastguards,' said Grey. Someone ran to do his bidding, and he turned to Sylvester.

'What's your friend up to?'

'I don't know,' said Sylvester, slowly, 'but if he doesn't get shot first, if anyone can bring that boat back safe, he can.' He looked around, noticing for the first time the absence of his cousin.

'Where's Merlin? Not staying at home like a good boy, surely.'

Grey looked at him. 'Your cousin is in hospital.' He said. 'In a coma from a massive drug overdose.' He paused. 'I'm sorry.'

Sylvester covered his face with his hands. 'Oh, God,' he said, and fell silent.

By common consent, those present who had nothing else to do immediately walked to the end of the quay and stood staring out to sea. Someone had a pair of binoculars, and passed them from hand to hand, but it was impossible to see what was happening. The cruiser, big as she was for her kind, was small out in that sea; she came and went among roaring waters, sometimes seeming to the watchers on the shore that she was totally overpowered. What was happening on board it was impossible to tell. Sylvester, standing helplessly among the policemen, felt himself grow older by the moment. He had grown extremely fond of Austine in the short time he had known her, Bob was an old friend, and Merlin – well, he was Merlin. Which, if any of the three of them, was going to come through this lot in one piece? Perhaps there would just be himself and Julie-Anne left to tell the tale...

'She's turning round!' called the man who held the binoculars. 'She's coming back!'

The wind howled around them as they stood and watched the gallant little craft rolling through that violent sea, each of them willing her safely to land. The waves seemed to tower over her from astern, threatening to swamp her as she ploughed valiantly towards the shore. One of two of them, it seemed to Sylvester, did swamp her. He closed his eyes, and found himself praying, desperately, unsuitably –

'*Our Father, which art in heaven, hallowed be thy name...*'

'What was that?' asked Grey.

The seas roared angrily on to the sandbank, spray drenched the watchers. The little boat was no longer so little, she was getting nearer, but it was easy to see that she was taking about all the punishment she could handle.

'I wouldn't be out there for anything you could give me,' said one of the policemen, awestruck. A welter of white foam broke over the cabin roof, and the boat wallowed, dangerously. It was possible to hear the engine now, in throbbing bursts above the whine of the wind and the crash of the waves. The entrance to the harbour, turbulent with foam, seemed to Sylvester's agonized eyes to be getting narrower and narrower. With that sea behind her to toss her in, would she make the harbour safely? Would she make it at all?

He spoke, without realizing he spoke aloud. 'Robert Chase, if you ever sailed to win, sail to win now. Win! Win! Win!'

The cruiser lurched dangerously towards the narrows, the big seas lifting her and throwing her about like driftwood. She was close in now, close enough for them to see Bob, intent at the wheel, every ounce or strength and skill and judgement that he possessed bent on bringing her safe home. The policeman, Davies, crouched in the well, blood streaming down his wet face, and at his feet, her head down out of the wind, soaked and scared, but alive, was Austine. Sylvester, seeing her there, could have shouted aloud had the situation not been too serious yet for such things.

A great wave, bigger than any yet, came rearing in from seaward, its face smooth and green and translucent, its curling top crinkled with foam. Sweeping inshore it came, curling wickedly as if to engulf the little boat, breaking with a welter of foam that swept over the quay with a force that made the watchers stagger. There was a moment of confusion, and then, as the men shook the water out of their eyes and looked about them, a shout went up.

She was not the trim little craft that had set out into that dreadful sea, but as she limped into harbour there was not a man there who did not greet her with admiration. She slid alongside the quay, and Sylvester jumped aboard to throw the mooring rope. A couple of detectives made it fast.

'Phew!' said Bob, dashing a hand across his eyes. 'These things aren't built for heavy seas!'

'Sail is the thing,' said Sylvester, and his voice was shaking.

'I don't think it's quite the day for it,' remarked Bob.

Eager hands lifted Austine and Constable Davies ashore; Davies looked in a bad way but Austine, although rather green in the face, appeared, mercifully, unhurt. She fell into Sylvester's waiting arms without a word, and clung to him. Finn seemed to have fared worst; he lay in a heap on the floorboards and hardly seemed to breathe.

'What happened?' asked Grey, looking down at him. 'How did you get him? What did you do?'

'Nothing,' said Bob, looking up from where he was fastening the stern warp. 'It didn't seem necessary – I just left it to nature. He couldn't manage the boat with one hand out there, so he had to put the gun down – I'm sorry, he shot your policeman first, but I couldn't really stop him – but the sea did the rest. He couldn't cope. It was as simple as that.'

'The Lord be thanked,' said Grey, soberly, and meant it.

Finn turned out to have fractured his skull when the vengeful seas threw him down, but he would live to stand his trial, with his friend Boswell, for murder and drug smuggling.

'Worse things could have happened to him,' said Superintendent Gardner, when he heard the news. 'A couple of Mick's sidekicks have been followed as far as Ipswich. They're getting near.'

Maitland, to whom he was speaking, looked wistful. 'Couldn't we arrange for him to escape? The punishment the law gives is so pansy nowadays.'

'Hmmm,' said the Superintendent, but made no further comment.

When it was all over, Sylvester drove Bob and Austine back to Raven's Dyke. Merlin's car was parked outside the door, with Julie-Anne just climbing out of it. She came slowly over to them.

'Austine?' she said, and then she saw her sister, scruffy and untidy, dressed in a weird collection of clothes borrowed from one of the policewomen to replace her own soaking wet ones, but alive and well. She was no longer that awful seasick green, but along with the rest of them, it would be a while before she would be herself again.

'Are you all right?' asked Julie-Anne.

'She's fine,' said Sylvester, jumping down and coming over to Julie-Anne. 'Merlin. What about him?'

'He's all right, too,' said Julie-Anne. 'At least, he will be when he's slept it off…he didn't get it all, or he'd be dead.'

Reaction caught Sylvester off his guard; he began to laugh.

'How heroic can you get!' he managed to say, between bursts of laughter. 'All this happening, Bob and Austine nearly drowned, dangerous criminals running amok all over the place – and Merlin gets himself put to sleep and misses the lot! That beats everything!'

Julie-Anne took his arm. Shaken herself, she recognized his outburst for what it was, the protest of overstrung nerves.

'Come indoors,' she said. 'Let's go and see if Sir Richard can raise some drinks – I, for one, need one!'

Then, at last, the nightmare was over and they were on their way south. Sylvester and Austine had taken the Land Rover and gone on ahead, absorbed and happy with each other; Bob drove Merlin's car and followed behind with the others. Merlin, having recovered from the hangover to end all hangovers, was quiet and subdued, and Julie-Anne, sitting in the back of the car looking lovingly at the back of his head, went cold all over when she thought of the narrowness of his escape. As they drove away from Raven's Dyke, she felt as if a great weight had rolled off her shoulders; it was over, and better that way, she supposed, than left to haunt them in the background, for had matters not come to a head it would have been difficult, if not impossible, to be properly casual about faceless bodies, but it had been a near thing, too near for comfort, and for herself, she did not think she would every wholly get over it. Although she might yet lose him, in one sense, to his girlfriend Winkie MacKenzie, even that would not be so hard to bear now; a world in which he did not even exist was unthinkable.

The journey was long and wearisome; Julie-Anne sat in the back of the car watching the scenery flying past, listening with only half an ear to the quiet conversation of the two men, talking together, as old friends will, about things which concerned them both, things and people of which she knew nothing. It seemed so long since she had known and loved her guardian, she thought, but what did she really know about him? At Raven's Dyke they had been out of the world, caught in a web of unnatural circumstances, each one of them behaving out of character, isolated in their private world of fear. What was he like among his own friends, in his own world? So very dear to her, and yet a stranger still, bound by friendships and loyalties of far longer standing than his acquaintance with herself and Austine. A whole lifetime of unknown friends surrounded him. How could anyone love so wholeheartedly, a person of whom they knew so little? She did not know, but she knew that whatever lay ahead now, even should she marry another man, a piece of her would always belong to him.

They picked their way through London and then at last they were on the home stretch. The car sped faster, as if it smelt its stable, through quiet green countryside, rolling fields, little villages and larger towns, southwards, ever southwards to the milder, warmer lands of the south west, until at last, as the dusk was falling, they drove over a stretch of downland within sight of the sea and rain into the outskirts of a little grey town lying sheltered in a fold of the low hills, and after twists and turns through built-up streets of shops and houses finally drew up outside a house in a street that appeared to back on to a river. The Land Rover was parked in the drive outside the doors of an enormous shed, and above the doors a signboard proclaimed the still unfamiliar legend, CHASE & RAVENSCOURT: BOATBUILDERS.

'Coming in for a minute?' asked Bob, preparing to leave them.

'No, thanks,' said Merlin. 'We'll go on. I'll see you tomorrow – and thanks.'

Bob went up the drive with a final wave, and Merlin slid across to the driving seat.

'Coming in the front, or staying there?' he asked Julie-Anne.

Julie-Anne elected for the front, and when she was settled they moved off again. Out of the town, away from the sea, through more of that gentle, green country, shadowed now as the night drew in and lights twinkled out in the cottages along the way.

'Nearly home now,' said Merlin, stealing a glance at his companion as they sped along. She smiled at him.

'Home – that sounds wonderful!'

The headlights picked up a sign at the side of the road: SHEARWATER 1½ m, and a little while later they ran into the narrow street of a little village, whisked through it, and slowed down outside a pair of huge wrought-iron gates set in a high stately wall. As they turned in between the pillars, crowned with heraldic beasts, the headlights flickered across grass and trees, and Julie-Anne gained an impression of space and green, growing things. A small lodge, like a miniature castle, appeared on their left and fell behind them as the long drive rolled under their wheels. A good half mile they must have gone, Julie-Anne estimated, and then suddenly, round a curve of a drive, there was the house lit up and welcoming, and she caught her breath.

It was beautiful; even in the dark it was possible to see how beautiful: long and gracious, high chimneys showing against the paler sky, pitched roofs in elegant symmetry, and tall windows glowing with friendly lights. Anything more unlike Raven's Dyke would have been impossible to find. The great front door stood open in welcome, and she could see Austine and Sylvester standing there, waiting for them. If it had been a nightmare before, this was a dream…a dream from which it would be a shame to wake.

Inside, the house continued to delight; everything in it was perfect, unostentatiously exactly right, and to Julie-Anne, used to a reasonable amount of monied luxury herself, even a little awe-inspiring. There was money around here, there was no doubt at all; she remembered hearing that old Lord Storre had made a fortune in oil somewhere, and seeing his lovely house, she could believe it. She wondered if Merlin had come into any of it when his uncle had died, and was immediately ashamed of herself. On the whole, she thought not, he had an air of self-sufficiency and ordinariness that did not go with all this quiet wealth.

The rest of the family came to meet her: the present Lord Storre, Sylvester's nephew Robin, a youth of fourteen or so with the dark-lashed, grey Ravenscourt eyes and untidy light brown hair and a friendly smile- anything less like her idea of an English lord would be hard to imagine, and his mother's parents, who were his guardians until he came of full age, an unconsciously gracious couple who made Julie-Anne feel an honoured guest, but also realize why Merlin had not sent them straight to his home.

Merlin had gone to put the car away, and Austine took her sister upstairs.

'What price Raven's Dyke now?' she asked, triumphantly, throwing open a door on the wide landing. 'How's that?'

'Pow!' exclaimed Julie-Anne. 'This is more like it!'

The room was large and light and beautiful; thick cream carpet, golden maple furniture, blue flowered counterpanes on the twin beds, blue velvet curtains at the tall window.

'And our own bathroom!' said Austine, opening another door. 'And a dressing-room, and about ten different towels, all reeking of glorious luxury! I didn't even have to unpack, a maid did it for me!' She sat down in a big arm-chair, and flung her arms wide. 'It was still light when we got here, and Sylvester took me round the stables – what horses, Julie, you never saw anything like them! And the grounds! It's glorious place!'

Julie-Anne went over to the window and drew back the curtain. Outside it was too dark to see very much, but she could imagine all the things that Austine was eagerly telling her about. A glorious place indeed – for a few short weeks. Then what?

A glorious place indeed in which to break one's heart...?

XII

'Long expected, one-and-twenty
Lingering year, at length is flown.'
Samuel Johnson: One-and-Twenty

Life at Ravenscourt Place proved a considerable contrast to life at Raven's Dyke. The great house and its grounds were as far removed as they could be from the architecturally beautiful, but decaying, moated grange in Suffolk; Mr and Mrs Fanshawe and young Lord Storre charming and attentive hosts in direct contrast to the absent-minded Sir Richard. The excellently discreet service, the immaculate estate, the glorious comfort and luxury of the house, were balm to spirits depressed by floods, dust, dim lights and the rough-and-ready methods of the Bartles – never mind all the murder and mayhem. Julie-Anne and Austine began to have different ideas of this England that had given them such a hard initial reception.

It was different, of course. For one thing, Merlin, once he had been passed as fit by the family doctor ('What did you give him?' asked Sylvester. 'You still sound like sandpaper to me.' To which Merlin replied that Dr Finn's final remedy, though drastic, had worked wonders!), was gone to work long before the girls got up for breakfast, and did not return until nearly dinner time, and Sylvester, too, was away at work for nearly as long a time each day. This meant that Julie-Anne and Austine had time on their hands during the daylight hours, but with a map, a hired car, and a resplendent picnic basket, they did not suffer from boredom. They very soon discovered that neither Merlin nor Sylvester considered an evening sitting at home with the telly as well spent, and very seldom remained on the premises after dinner. It was Sylvester that took the girls out most often, to the pictures, or dancing, usually in company with friends of his.

Merlin seemed content to let him do so; where he went, and what he did, he kept his own affair. Julie-Anne wondered if he was out somewhere with Winkie, but felt that she could hardly ask.

As the weeks went slowly by, Austine and Julie-Anne learned a little more about their guardian. He and Sylvester did not seem to share the same circle of friends, although both of them belonged to the same sailing club in a nearby village called Emberton, situated on the banks of Embridge Harbour — into which, at the eastern end, ran the river Alder for which Aldmere was named — and, so said Sylvester, bringing his local-geography lesson to an end, generally went down there together during the summer, although not literally together as Merlin sailed with Bob, of course, and Sylvester, who had a racing dinghy of his own — although in a different and rather less exciting class — went his own way with his own friends on these occasions.

Merlin did take the girls down to this club one Sunday lunchtime and showed them Bob's boat, sleek, delicate and insubstantial, with graceful, rakish lines. Her name was *Scary Mary*, and she was the apple of Bob's eye. Merlin had other interests too, they soon discovered; for one thing he was a stereo hound, with a rather advanced taste in music, which he liked loud. Between the boat and the hi-fi, Julie-Anne began to see that her love could prove heavy going if not properly handled, but she did not love him any the less. In fact, as day followed day, she found she loved him more and more, which was awkward, because he treated her with no more than the brotherly affection that he accorded to his true sister, and she could not flatter herself that there was any sign of anything warmer.

They met Winkie, of course, one Saturday night when Merlin and Sylvester took them both to a dance down at the sailing club. She was a tall, slim, dark girl with a tranquil disposition and a quiet sense of humour; between her and Merlin was the ease of old acquaintance but, it seemed to Julie-Anne, a certain amount of restraint as well. Perhaps she was kidding herself, she told herself firmly. No good imagining things to suit herself, but there was no doubt that, on that night at least, Merlin devoted himself to his wards, and Winkie, although part of the circle, could not be said to be with him. Bob was present too, that evening, with his wife and a good many other people whose names and faces Julie-Anne afterwards found it hard to remember clearly. Austine and Sylvester had drifted away before the night was over and joined another set of people around the bar; it became gradually borne in on Julie-Anne that the crowd with whom she found herself were the elite of the club, a surmise borne out by the Roll of Honour out in the entrance hall, which bore the names and achievements of the club's more glorious members, and on which the name of Chase, particularly, seemed more than ordinarily prominent. For his skill and seamanship under power, indeed, she had too much reason to be grateful to call it in doubt under sail, even without written proof. It surprised her a little to discover that Merlin was the club secretary, and possibly explained where he vanished to of an evening. He certainly had a many-faceted personality, but then she had guessed that from the start. She was interested to find him much liked by his peers, and standing in no one's shadow.

It was a lovely evening altogether, and the first time she felt that she could say that she was truly 'taken out' by Merlin, but she was left feeling that he had done it as a duty, because he was her guardian, and although he had enjoyed it (she hoped), he was in no particular hurry to repeat the performance. At least he had held her in his arms, she consoled herself, even if it was only to dance with her. Pleasant it had been, too.

Austine's future had been the subject of a certain amount of discussion; it was almost settled that she was to try for a place at the nearest training hospital and be a nurse; Julie-Anne privately wondered if it was worth it for she and Sylvester appeared to have a good thing going, and although Austine was young yet she was by no means as young for her age as she had been before her experiences at Raven's Dyke. About Julie-Anne, nothing further had been said. She mentioned once that she thought she might go back to the States, but the only response this carefully trialed red herring had elicited from her guardian was unsatisfactory.

'Why not, if you want to?' he said. 'We'll see, shall we?' Which could mean anything – or nothing.

A week before Julie-Anne's twenty-fourth birthday, Merlin had a letter from Hubert Lacey; Mr Achenbaum was coming over to England to represent the trustees of the estate, and to see about the winding up of the trust in respect of Julie-Anne's share. He flew over from the States, and had to be invited to Ravenscourt Place, an invitation that of course he accepted. Julie-Anne half thought that she would go back with him when he left; there did not appear to be anything to stay for.

She awoke on the morning of her birthday feeling unsuitably depressed. Merlin had had a day off work the previous day, and he and Mr Achenbaum had spent most of the day in the Estate Office, sorting out business and talking – heaven knew what about. Julie-Anne herself had had a talk with Mr Achenbaum before going to bed, mainly about Austine, and she had been left with the feeling that she was being all wound up and done with and cast adrift to fend for herself. The feeling had persisted through the night until the morning, hence the depression.

'Happy birthday, darling Julie!' said Austine, sitting up in bed. The sun was shining, and the birds twittering, and it was so balmy outside it was almost possible to imagine spring was on its way. Not a day for being miserable. Julie-Anne took a hold on herself. It couldn't be so bad, really. She could bring her holiday to a close and go home to all her old friends, and leave Austine happy and cared for; there was nothing to be sorry for herself about in that.

'Thank you,' she said. Austine looked at her severely.

'What is the matter with you?' she demanded. 'You've been going steadily downhill all week! What is it – old age, or what?'

Julie-Anne had to laugh; Austine looked so funny with her cross face, and her hair all on end.

'Maybe it is, at that,' she said. 'All those chances missed and gone under the bridge, and me an old maid. Take no notice.'

Austine looked at her under her eyelashes.

'You should have made a play for my brother and been a sister to me all over again,' she said. 'Why don't you? There's time yet – if you ask me, he'd be a pushover.'

'He would?' asked Julie-Anne, staring at her. 'You could have fooled me!'

'No need,' said Austine, getting out of bed and heading for the bathroom. 'You can fool yourself all that's needed.'

The door banged behind her, and Julie-Anne looked at it thoughtfully. What had she meant by that, if anything?

On the way down to breakfast, she ran into Merlin in the hall, on the way to work. He paused to give her a brotherly kiss and wish her a happy birthday before dashing out of the door with a hurried 'See you later.' Not very lover-like, so whatever Austine had meant, she couldn't mean that.

Sylvester, on the other hand, had deferred his departure for the architects' office where he worked, and was waiting to give her a proper greeting and a present – two presents, in fact. One of them was a very pretty bracelet, the other was a book on learning to sail.

'What do I want that for?' asked Julie-Anne, looking at it. 'Not that it's not very nice, of course,' she added, hastily.

'I just thought that it might come in handy sometime,' said Sylvester, airily. 'If you're staying among us, you're bound to take to the water sooner or later.'

Mr Achenbaum had a present for her too: a bottle of outrageously expensive scent with love from himself and his wife, and a box of chocolates from Lacey. Austine donated an expensive cashmere sweater that Julie-Anne had seen and fallen in love in the shop in Aldmere, and a necklace and earrings to match Sylvester's bracelet. The post brought floods of cards from friends in America, and from new friends made since their arrival at Ravenscourt Place, and even one from Sir Richard, reminding her unpleasantly of things she would have sooner forgotten. The parcel post, later in the day, brought a silk scarf and more chocolates from Anabel, who made a pose of never forgetting a birthday, but in reality employed a secretary to remember for her. Julie-Anne wondered, fleetingly, if she ever remembered her son's birthday – and when it was. There was still a tremendous lot she didn't know about him, and which it looked as if she would never learn now.

The two girls went out to lunch with Mr Achenbaum. He wanted to know what had been happening to them since their arrival in England, and they gave him a somewhat expurgated account of their stay in Suffolk, which he did not find amusing.

However, 'I knew you shouldn't have come on your own,' was all that he said, recognizing, no doubt, that nobody did that sort of thing on purpose. They talked about Austine for a while, covering old ground, and then Mr Achenbaum turned to Julie-Anne.

'And you?' he said. 'You're free now, to do what you like, and marry who you will. Any plans?'

'I'm going to marry a fortune hunter and have ten children,' said Julie-Anne, a shade defiantly. He nodded genially.

'That sounds an excellent idea. Any particular fortune hunter in mind?' His eyes were twinkling as he spoke, and for the third time that day a small doubt crept into Julie-Anne's mind. Something was wrong here, but she could not put her finger on it. What had he and Merlin been talking about for so long yesterday?

Her heart gave a sudden thump and began to race madly, and she felt her colour rise. Fool! She felt Austine's eyes on her, and she was smiling too.

'No particular one,' she said. 'Any old layabout will do.'

He hadn't even given her a birthday present, and they had only met in the hall by mistake. Not to mention all those weeks of brotherliness. A girl didn't marry her brother.

'Ah well, we'll see,' said Mr Achenbaum, as Merlin had before him.

They drove home after a very splendid lunch, and as they came up the drive Julie-Anne was surprised to see Merlin's car parked outside the house. He shouldn't be home for hours yet. A perfectly groundless fear that he had been taken ill at work took hold of her, and she tumbled headlong out of the car only to be pulled up short because Austine was grinning at her.

'I'm going to take Mr Achenbaum for a walk in the park,' she said, 'Coming?'

'I don't think so, thank you,' said Julie-Anne, and went indoors. The great hallway with its black-and-white marble floor, glowing woodwork, and polished suits of armour, and the more-than-adequate, un-Raven's Dyke-ish fire blazing in the beautiful marble fireplace, was deserted. It was far too big a house to go hunting for people in, apart from the fact that Merlin could also be anywhere in a few thousand acres of land, and of course, probably had no desire to see her anyway, but of that fact she was no longer sure. Too many other people seemed to have other ideas, unless she was imagining things.

She found him in the long gallery that was hung from end to end with pictures of Ravenscourts dead and gone. Sylvester's brother, Timothy, the last heir, who had never succeeded to the title, was the last in the line; he had been a lot older than Sylvester, but he was very like him. Merlin, in person, was by the big window, looking out over the park, his back towards her. A red carpet ran the length of the gallery and, walking along it, she came up to him without his hearing.

'Hello,' said Julie-Anne. 'What brought you back?'

Merlin had jumped away from the window as if he had been shot. 'Don't creep up on me like that!' he exclaimed. 'You nearly gave me heart failure!'

'I saw your car,' said Julie-Anne. 'I wondered if you were all right.'

'Good heavens, yes! No one has tried to murder me for ages. I came back to see you.'

'Me?' said Julie-Anne.

'Mmm. Why not?'

'You saw me this morning,' Julie-Anne reminded him.

'Yes, I know I did. It didn't quite seem the moment, somehow.'

'Moment for what?'

'For anything. I was going to catch you when I got home this evening, but after I'd ruined a perfectly good sheet of marine ply, and nearly had Bob's fingers off in the bandsaw, I thought it wouldn't wait that long... so I came back...as you see.'

'No,' said Julie-Anne. 'I don't see.'

'Well...' Merlin looked at her ruefully. 'Oh, Julie, do try! I'm not your guardian anymore.'

'No – ' said Julie-Anne with difficulty.

'So – now you know me a bit better – are you still of the same mind?'

'The same mind – ' began Julie-Anne, but nothing came out. She cleared her throat. 'The same mind as what?'

Merlin reached out and took her hands. 'I thought you loved me,' he said, simply. 'Don't – please – tell me I was just being conceited.'

'Oh...no!' said Julie-Anne. 'But I thought – you didn't – I mean – '

'How could I?' asked Merlin, understanding her perfectly. 'You were my ward, I was supposed to guard you from people like me.'

'No,' said Julie-Anne. 'Not people like you. Daddy trusted you.'

'That's what Mr Achenbaum said yesterday.'

'You...asked him?'

'Well, yes. Do you mind? He's the nearest thing you have left to a relation, for you can't count my mother. I didn't feel prepared to wait another minute but somehow – I couldn't just sign my guardianship away and – well, it was awkward.'

'What did he say?' asked Julie-Anne.

'Bless you, my children, or words to that effect. But what are *you* going to say?'

'To what?' asked Julie-Anne. She was beginning to recover from the shock, and the thought of the miserable weeks she had spent since she met him came back to her. He had probably suffered too, but nevertheless he was not going to get away with it that easily. She said so.

'After all these weeks,' she said. 'What do you think I've been feeling like?' And you didn't even get me a birthday card, never mind a present.'

'Oh, I remembered the present,' said Merlin. 'I just wasn't sure that you'd want it.'

This was outrageous. Julie-Anne frowned at him. 'What about Winkie?' she asked, determined to make him beg for quarter somehow. 'Sylvester said – '

'Sylvester can talk a lot of rubbish, but as a matter of fact, in that instance he was right. I asked Winkie if she'd marry me at Christmas – she said, "Not on your life", or something that meant it. The minute you walked in my bedroom door, I was never more thankful for anything in my life.'

Julie-Anne gave it up; he was obviously past praying for. 'I love you,' she said, simply.

'Enough to marry me? I'm not in the least bit wealthy, and my friends tell me I can be a pain about the place. But I love you very dearly and if you could...I'd count it an honour...'

'Oh, Merlin, or course I will,' said Julie-Anne.

He found her present later; a ring with a single sapphire set in a delicate diamond star.

'I hope you like it,' he said, diffidently. 'I know girls are supposed to like to choose their own engagement rings, but it seemed right for you somehow...'

'I love it,' said Julie-Anne, adding, suspiciously, 'How did you get the size right?'

Merlin looked slightly embarrassed. 'I pinched that one of Austine's you keep borrowing,' he confessed. 'She didn't miss it – and I didn't have it for long.'

Julie-Anne began to laugh. 'You're incredible!' she said. 'I'm beginning to think I don't know you at all!' She looked down at the ring, and suddenly said, 'Sylvester gave me a book on sailing – I wondered...'

'Sylvester isn't the fool I take him for sometimes,' said Merlin. He slipped his arm around her shoulders and drew her to him.

'Come on,' he said, a few satisfying minutes later. 'Let's go tell them all.'

'Just one thing,' said Julie-Anne, looking up at him lovingly. 'I ought to warn you, I suppose...'

'Warn me?'

'I want ten children,' said Julie-Anne.

Merlin raised his eyebrows. 'Ten, darling?' he asked.

'Ten,' said Julie-Anne, firmly.

'Oh well,' said Merlin, leading her along the gallery towards the stairs. 'On your money we can afford them. So be it.'

Julie-Anne gave him up. He was obviously quite beyond redemption, and she loved every unregenerate inch of him.

He was definitely far and away the best birthday present that she had ever had.

Lightning Source UK Ltd.
Milton Keynes UK
UKHW020720210622
404740UK00012B/1308